ONE
OF
THE
CHOSEN

ONE
OF
THE
CHOSEN

by Danuta Gleed

Edited by
Frances Itani and Susan Zettell

BuschekBooks

Canadian Cataloguing in Publication Data

Gleed, Danuta, 1946-1996
    One of the chosen

Short stories.
ISBN 0-9699904-3-X

    I. Itani, Frances, 1942-   II. Zettell, Susan, 1951-
III. Title

PS8563.L43O54 1997   C813'.54   C97-900710-0
PR9199.3.G578O54 1997

Acknowledgements

"Bones." *The Windsor Review*. Vol. 28, No. 1, Spring 1995, and finalist in *The Journey Prize Anthology*. Toronto: McClelland & Stewart, 1996.
"Evening in Paris." Prize winner in the 1990 Short Fiction Contest, *Prism International*. Vol. 29, No. 3, Spring 1991.
"Nest." *Blood & Aphorisms*. No. 7, Summer 1992, and in *Stories from Blood & Aphorisms*. Toronto: Steel Rail Publishing/Gutter Press, 1993.
"One of the Chosen." Prize winner in the 1991 Short Fiction Contest, *Prism International*. Vol. 30, No. 3, Spring 1992.
"Saturday." *NeWest Review*. Vol. 19, No. 1, October/November 1993.
"The Mango Tree." *The Canadian Forum*. Vol. LXXV, No. 859, May 1997.

Printed by Hignell Printing Limited, Winnipeg, Manitoba
Book design: Marie Tappin

BuschekBooks
PO Box 74053
35 Beechwood Avenue
Ottawa, Ontario K1M 2H9
Editor: John Buschek

TABLE OF CONTENTS

INTRODUCTION

I am a visitor in Danuta's home on Salt Spring Island and it is six months after Danuta's death. As I write, I am distracted by her stunning view of Moresby Island and Swanson Channel, by the pair of eagles that swoop down from their nest to fish in the bay, by the wind as it shifts the leaves of the arbutus outside her window, by the sound of the waves as they beat the shore in her cove. *It's perfect for writing*, Danuta had told me. *You'll have to come and visit.*

Danuta and her husband built the B.C. house in 1996. It was a place Danuta loved and to which she intended to move permanently, from her Ottawa home.

In the mid 1980s when Frances Itani first told me about Danuta, a student in her writing class at the University of Ottawa, Danuta was fighting for her life in hospital, near death with lupus. A year later, I joined Danuta's writing group. She would bring her complex, sad stories to us, always tentative, always self-critical. *It's no good*, she'd say. *It's not finished. I'm not happy with it.*

Danuta's illness became more and more incapacitating. Though frail, she remained characteristically feisty. She wrote less, but continued to improve her stories. On a trip to Britain she spent time with her mother and her beloved Auntie, recording their recollections of Siberia, the long trek to Africa, their eventual emigration to England. In 1995 Danuta was hospitalized and I offered to help gather her stories together into a manuscript. She accepted, but we struggled to find time. I mentioned the project to Frances, who offered her expertise. *Let's get this thing done*, Frances said.

Before Danuta left for Salt Spring Island in August 1996, we decided, come hell or high water, that when she returned to Ottawa in the spring we would get the stories ready for publication. Danuta never came back. She died in December.

On Danuta's bookshelf on Salt Spring Island, I find Eudora Welty's *The Eye of the Story*, and open the book at a dog-eared page where this passage is marked:

> It seems likely that all of one writer's stories do tend to spring from the same source within.... However they differ in theme or approach, however they vary in mood or fluctuate in their strength, their power to reach the mind or heart, all of one writer's stories carry their signature because of the one impulse most characteristic of [her]...own gift—to praise, to love, to call up to view.

It has been my privilege to realize Danuta's gift and, with Frances, to call it up to view.

Susan Zettell
Salt Spring Island, June 1997

—

From the beginning, the shaping of this book (the result of several people's efforts) has been a work of love. Over a period of several months, Susan Zettell and I, as editors, would read through the material separately and then meet to discuss. We met frequently. As there were sometimes as many as four undated versions per story, our first task was to choose what we believed to be the best of each draft. No problem there; we agreed, first time, in every instance. Much more difficult were the decisions about what to include from the greater fabric of unformed and fragmented material. To arrive at the hundred or so pages in this book, we read perhaps six times that number.

I'd had the privilege of looking over Danuta's shoulder as mentor for a number of years, and some of the stories were familiar to me. Others were a surprise. As I read, I began to settle into the detailed, sensuous world of the post WWII refugee camps in Africa. The world of the watchful child who never stopped asking questions, the child who learned that the truth could be known in different versions. Danuta lived her own life with courage, and she explored courage and displacement as themes in her fiction. She had much to share, and while she was learning to find her material, so also was she learning to craft it into story.

Of the nine stories, six were published, including "Nest," and "Saturday," two of the earliest. Several were prize-winners. "The Mango Tree," published in *The Canadian Forum* after Danuta's death, was the only story that required substantial editing. We had to join the one ending (found in three old versions) to the first section—discovered in a more recent draft. "Running Away" and "Nairobi" were not entirely finished and I'm certain that Danuta would have written several more drafts. Because they were close to completion and contributed to the uniqueness of the book, we decided to include them as they were. We tried as much as possible to honour Danuta's intent and to keep editorial changes to a minimum.

I am grateful to John Gleed, Rachel and Jonathan, for access to Danuta's papers. I thank John Buschek, who approached us and offered to publish this book, and who has included us at every stage of its production. Sincere thanks, also, to Sharon Butala and Audrey Thomas.

Finally, I come to the end of this project with mixed feelings. I am glad to have had a part in bringing forth the book Danuta struggled to create through years of health and years of severe illness. It is with sorrow that I lose a friend, a gifted writer who had begun to allow her material to speak and who created exquisitely layered stories such as "One of the Chosen," and "Summer Fair." It is unfortunate that the bulk of her private writing will never be read.

Nonetheless, within the finished material, the depth of Danuta's artistry, the complexity of her writer's vision, the colour and light of her own transformed African childhood, add riches to our body of Canadian literature. Indeed, many of the stories included here are testament to Danuta Gleed's power to reach inside and touch us at both mind and heart.

Frances Itani
Ottawa, June 1997

BONES

Sophie wraps the watercolour in a shiny paper striped pink and silver. She plants a pink bow, round and wide as a grapefruit, on top. She plans to carry it as hand luggage tomorrow, to keep it safe and to protect the wrapping from getting crushed. This painting pleases her: the waves brushed by a silver light, the red stains in the foreground and, in the centre, a splatter of yellow, a point at which the sun may have recently set or where something–or someone–has fallen. A half-moon, transparent as a fingernail, sits in the top left-hand corner. On the bottom, centre, she has printed *Sunset*, so Janet, her mother, for whom the gift is intended, will at least have an idea.

"Happy birthday," Sophie will murmur as she holds out the gift. The wrapping paper, the bow, are things Janet is sure to admire. She'll trace the bow with a short, red-tipped fingernail, thoughtfully, while Sophie peers into the fridge for celery, green peppers, carrots, sour cream and packets of leek and onion soup for the dips. Bill, Sophie's stepfather, will be clattering about outside with the barbecue and the chairs and tables for the birthday celebration. When Sophie turns around, Janet's eyes will be dark in her white face.

Sophie is sure of this. She has become quite the expert.

Soon after her impulsive move to the west coast five years ago, Sophie's paintings began to emerge quickly, one barely completed before another took shape. Like snapshots. Back east, she struggled over pictures of gardens crammed with sunflowers, slender white lilies and fat roses. She painted robins and blue jays, small children in yellow bonnets building castles on the beach, a sun as round and sweet as an orange spinning in the sky. Everything light, bright, so perfect.

Now, in her studio apartment on the top floor of a creaky house, she stares at each completed watercolour in wonder, as if she doesn't know what she has painted or whether she has, indeed, painted it herself. She thinks about this development at times. Distance, she assumes, has somehow shifted her perspective. Or has she been hypnotized by the sharp air, the mountains, the ocean? Or the sunlight that fills the skylight on clear days? On dull days, raindrops race across. Some nights, the skylight is flooded with stars. But she doesn't care too much about the answer. And why, she asks herself, as long as the paintings keep coming, should she?

The first painting emerged within two days of her arrival, while boxes and suitcases were still stacked against the wall. Leafless, crooked black trees emerged beneath her brush, trapped in a cold blue and white fog. There was a figure, or a shadow, beyond the trees.

Winter, she printed at the bottom of the painting when it was completed. She sat back. Well, she whispered. Well.

Winter was the first painting Sophie presented to Janet as a birthday gift. Next year there was *Water*. *Fire* and *Night Sky* followed. All have disappeared. When Sophie asks about them, Janet claims she has packed them in boxes and stored them in a dark, dry spot in the basement to keep them safe. They may be valuable one day, she adds as she stares at Sophie in a bemused way.

"Have you ever thought of painting something different?" she asks. "Something bright and cheerful. You know, like the stuff you did before?"

Sophie pretends to think this question over.

In Janet's and Bill's house, framed yellow and orange blooms hang above the living room fireplace. A cluster of white sailboats skims across a too-blue lake above the sideboard. A young girl with yellow ribbons in her hair and lace around her collar sits inside an ornate golden frame in the hall.

Janet's question does not offend Sophie. She sees it instead as proof that though Janet feigns indifference, the dark colours and odd, vague shapes she paints do disturb her. This makes Sophie smile.

"All I do is reproduce the recurring images that appear in my head," she replies. She spreads her hands in a gesture that could pass for helplessness and adds, "And it happens to be a lucky coincidence that people open their wallets wide for them."

"Modern art," Janet sighs. "I'll never understand it."

Sophie draws the curtains, slips into her nightdress. Tickets, gift, clothes for tomorrow, book for the plane, she counts in her head. In the kitchen, she pours the orange juice and milk down the drain. She moves to the living room, picks up the paper that has been lying on the table all day, smooths it, reads for the tenth or twentieth time the brief article squeezed into a corner of the back page.

Man Carries Human Bones in Suitcase

A thirty-three-year-old man from India was stopped by security guards at the airport in Tel Aviv when an X-ray machine revealed he was carrying items in his suitcase that were first believed to be weapons. On closer examination, the suitcase was found to contain a complete human skeleton. The man claimed that these were the bones of his father. He intended to keep travelling with them until he found a suitable place to settle, he explained. He then planned to bury his father nearby. Authorities are investigating.

Sophie cuts out the article, slips it into her wallet. From the moment she first read it, she has wanted to know what has *not* been reported. She wants to know *why* and *how*. Did this man have some special bond with his father or did he feel guilt for something he did—or omitted to do? And how did he get the bones in the first place? Did he dig up his father's grave? Or worse? How much worse could it be?

She imagines again the shocked faces of the security guards, the agitation of this man, this son, as he fiddles with the locks on the suitcase. Drops of sweat the size of pinheads gather above his top lip. Damp hair sticks to his forehead. Because of some petty rule or regulation, the father he has tucked away for safekeeping may now be taken from him. His hands begin to shake and he turns to look for help.

People gather, stare. When the suitcase is finally flung open, they whisper, smirk their embarrassment and horror behind their hands.

Sophie is certain that had she been there, she would have smiled her support at the man. She would have cheered him on because at least this devoted—or foolish—son knows something important. He knows where his father is, which is something she has not known about her own father, for years. Twenty-five years, precisely.

All *she* knows is that her father is somewhere. Dead or alive, he is somewhere. Because even the dead take up space.

There are times when Sophie thinks she makes her father up, conjures him the way a magician pulls a rabbit from an empty hat, a row of coloured squares of fabric from his sleeve. But when she turns to the one photograph she has—proof—which now stands on a table by the window next to a pot of purple African violets, she knows.

In the photograph, her father has a smooth face and dark eyes. He is wearing a uniform: baggy pants tucked into boots up to his ankles, a shirt that appears to be made of rough cloth, a flat cap cocked sideways on his head. The shirt has a collar so high it seems to be choking him. When Sophie was a girl, her father pointed out to her the brass buttons on the shirt, the new, polished boots. He shook his head as he told her he was proud the day the photograph was taken. He was a man, a soldier. He strutted about in his uniform, and his parents, his younger brothers and sisters, laughed and clapped. He was off to war, to save them.

But when Sophie looks at the photograph now, she can't see the man or the soldier. She sees only the stunned eyes of a boy. A boy who must pretend to be a man, so he can pretend to be a soldier.

She splashes water over her face, brushes her teeth, runs a comb through her hair. Quickly, quickly. If she stands in front of the mirror too long, she begins to see her father's pale face taking shape in the halo of her own black hair. Blank eyes, waxy skin, thinned lips. The image blurs, recedes.

A trick of the light, but that cannot be all. She is getting older and her features are settling into his. She is forty, the same age her father was when he disappeared. She lifts a single white hair among the black, twirls and twirls it around her forefinger.

She will pass smoothly through airport security, tomorrow. There is nothing suspicious in her suitcase or the canvas bag in which she will carry the watercolour, nothing startling or offensive.

The X-ray machine will pick up the metal frame of the picture in the bag. The bag will be unzipped, the gift removed. Probing fingers will move around the frame, lift the edge of the wrapping paper, gently, so as not to tear it. A nod, a glance at the solemn, dark-haired woman in sandals and loose cotton dress, and the gift will be returned.

Sophie will smile as she picks up her bag. No one could possibly mistake a gift wrapped in pink and silver paper and topped with a pink bow, for a weapon.

Another Friday night at seven, and Stefan, Sophie's father, pats his pockets for cigarettes and wallet, grabs his jacket from the hook behind the door. There's the crunch of a car on the gravel beside the cottage as soon as he leaves, the slam of doors, footsteps, raised voices, laughter. Janet's sisters—Betty and Sue—enter, faces half-hidden behind bags of groceries.

"Here." They thrust the bags at Sophie.

Janet prepares coffee, lays out plates for cake and cookies. A bottle of sherry appears.

The women settle around the table. They are broad and tall, their heads wild with pale curls. Their faces are pink, as if they have been scrubbed recently. They sit with thighs apart, broad feet planted on the floor, grip mugs and glasses with firm hands. They talk about the weather; who will make or bring what, for Janet's birthday barbecue on Sunday; the price of eggs or milk; the new kind of food mixer Betty bought at Sears; and, eventually, they talk about Stefan.

Sophie places milk, butter, juice, in the fridge. Tuna, cookies, cans of soup go in the top cupboard. She slams the cans down hard to drown out the sound of her father's name snagged in the voices behind her. Stefan. Stefan. Drinking again. Another job lost. Down to odd jobs now. Hardly enough to keep body and soul together. He'll never change, and you, Janet, will never have a home of your own. You'll be stuck in this miserable fam- ily cottage for ever.

Betty and Sue remind Janet they had warned her about those DPs who flooded the country after the war. They were not romantic or mysterious, as she wanted to believe. They were strange. That's all. Anyone could see that. Hollow-cheeked, in loose clothes scavenged from somewhere, the women in flat brown shoes and black headscarves, they prowled the streets, peered into store windows, into passing faces, as if they were starving.

"Oh, but there were good times," *Janet interrupts*. "At his friends' in the evening, a bottle of vodka passed around—I got to quite like it. We sat on crates, lit candles, smoked, talked. They sang, wonderful songs. I didn't understand the words but, you know, they sounded like hymns."

"Dirges," *Sue scoffs*.

"And Stefan," *Janet continues, her voice firm,* "Stefan brought me chocolates or, when he was broke, wild flowers. Those dark eyes—I swear he bewitched me. And how could I not feel sorry for him? Every single member of his family died of disease or starvation in that labour camp in Siberia the Russians dragged them to. Imagine. He cried when he told me. Every single one—parents, sisters, brothers. He was in the army then—he doesn't even know where they were buried. Must have been awful."

"It may be a horrible thing to say, but it might have been better all round if he'd gone, too," *Betty says. There's a hush, the scrape of a chair.* "Well, would you want to live if your whole family had gone? I wouldn't."

Sophie is kneeling on the counter, arranging cereal boxes in the top cupboard. She pauses, waiting for her mother's voice. She glances over her shoulder. Janet is twisting her glass between two fingers, staring into it as if she can see something significant inside.

Sophie folds the bags and slips them into the drawer.

"Good night. Good night." *She kisses each aunt on the cheek.*

"A bit early for bed, isn't it?" Sue asks.

"I'm going to read."

Sophie sits on the bed in her narrow room and stares at her reflection in the mirror. She wonders where her father is. He won't tell her where he goes on Friday nights from seven until eleven. He pats her on the head when she asks and tells her not to worry.

The voices of the women press in through the walls. How sure they always sound, Sophie thinks. How certain they are right. They make firm comments about everything—politicians, the state of the country, the state of the world. And people. "She has her father's nose, her mother's eyes," they say, as if a person is made up of puzzle pieces. "A high forehead, definitely his grandmother's." The sisters' comments about Stefan are made in louder, more confident voices. They could be doctors making a diagnosis.

Sophie leans towards the mirror. Her father's eyes, brown beads, stare back. Her hair is black, her face pale and long, like his. Mysterious, romantic. There is nothing of Janet in her, she realizes with satisfaction.

Ignore him, Janet had said one winter night as she sat over her embroidery, fashioning a garden of roses on the hem of a skirt while Stefan tramped outside through the snow in his slippers.

"He's upset," Sophie sobbed. "He'll freeze to death. We have to do something."

"He just wants attention." Janet snapped a thread with her teeth, a small, tight sound. "I can only stand so much, you know."

Sophie grabbed her coat, pulled on her boots and ran to the door. The cold pinched her face. Stefan was plodding through snow that reached to his knees, shirt sleeves rolled up, arms raised.

"Siberia! Siberia!" he yelled. "Bloody Siberia!" The words sliced the night.

Well, Sophie thought as she took his hand and led him back as if he were an obedient child. Well, she murmured. It could be Siberia, wherever, whatever it is. It could be. It's only a name, after all. Who has the right to say it's not?

"Let's go," Stefan says to Sophie late next day, the day before the birthday barbecue.

She rouses herself from the grass where she's flipping through a magazine. Her father slips a bottle into his pocket and marches ahead. She walks behind, swinging her arms. She hums as she watches Stefan's long strides. On days like this, she's sure he knows everything.

They veer off the path and tramp through bushes and trees. They stop, listen to the mutter of birds, squirrels, chipmunks. Stefan pulls out the bottle from his pocket, raises it high, a salute to the setting sun, and brings it to his lips.

"One day," he says, "I'll show you how to fish—in a proper lake, not this filthy river. I'll teach you which grzyby—mushrooms—are poisonous and which are not."

He parts long grass with a stick. He is looking for szczaw—a name he frowns over because he's unable to translate it. Green leaves, he explains, a bit like dandelion.

"We made szczaw soup at home," he tells Sophie. "It's wonderful. A bit sour, a bit sweet. It's good to know about these things in case you're stuck."

He grabs fistfuls of wild flowers—purple blue harebells, Queen Anne's lace, tall daisies. "They'll look fine on the picnic table at the barbecue tomorrow," he says.

Janet is a shadow bending over the vegetable garden when they return. She rises, holds out a tomato punctured with holes, and shakes her head.

Stefan thrusts the flowers towards her. "For you."

"Ah, Stefan. I can't cook these for dinner, now, can I? Can I?" she cries. She drops the flowers on the picnic table and runs into the cottage. They can see her in the kitchen window, a still silhouette in the light.

Stefan settles down on the dock. The sky is darkening. Sophie lowers herself beside him. He extends his hand towards the river, a benediction. The water is a dark, rippled skin. He points to the stars that arc boring pinpricks of light into the sky.

"And over there," he indicates a bright, steady glow, "a planet."

"Look at the moon," he says. "So round and smug. It's been there forever. When we're gone it will still be there. That moon-face sees everything. Sits and watches. Little things, big things. The white rabbit-tail that flits under a bush. The petals of a flower closing for the night. The man who brandishes a gun, a knife. Today. Yesterday, last year. One hundred, one thousand years ago."

Sophie looks up. The moon's face is still and solemn as a face on a coin. Stefan lifts his bottle to his lips. A frog croaks in the reeds. A breeze in a hurry rattles the leaves on the trees.

"There's no difference between the past and the present when the past is still going on in your head," Stefan says. He turns to Sophie, his face white in the dusk. "You must never forget. You won't forget, will you? Promise me."

"No." Sophie makes her voice firm. "No. I won't forget." She nods as she speaks because she wants him to know she is listening and that she wants to understand. Her bare feet slap the water. She wonders if he's joking and if she should laugh a little.

"Do you realize," Janet says to no one in particular at the barbecue next day, "that in two years I'll be forty? Forty! Half my life frittered away and nothing to show for it."

Sophie notices Betty and Sue exchange glances with their husbands. Janet places a slice of chocolate cake in front of Stefan. He lets his fork clatter onto the plate, rises and strolls towards the bush, his hands in his pockets.

"We'll clear up," Betty says as soon as everyone has finished. Sue is already stacking the plates.

Sophie takes Stefan's cake into the cottage, covers it with plastic wrap and leaves it in the fridge. Janet disappears into the bedroom, emerges with a suitcase as Sophie is washing the last bowl in the sink.

"Come on." She grips Sophie's wrist.

"Where to?"

"To Betty's. For a few days. Just you and me."

"What for?"

"I'll explain in the car."

"You go. I want to stay here."

"Sophie. You must come." Janet points towards the bush. "It's for his own good. He needs to sort himself out."

Sophie rubs a towel slowly between each finger while she thinks. Aunt Betty has a bungalow with a round swimming pool in the backyard. She has a bicycle Sophie is allowed to use whenever she visits and a TV in the living room and the spare bedroom. Sophie hangs the towel slowly on a hook.

"Can we come back soon to see if everything is all right?" she asks.

Janet nods.

The first day, Sophie takes her aunt's bicycle and cycles until her legs ache. She meets the girl across the road when she returns and invites her for a swim. Each morning they swim; then, they watch the soaps in the afternoon. They swoon and giggle when their favourite actor appears.

When they have been at Betty's for ten days, Sophie decides she doesn't want to see the girl across the road any more. She's too tired. She changes into her swimsuit and swims round and round the pool alone. She imagines she's a goldfish and the thought makes her laugh and cry at the same time.

She makes Janet promise they'll drop in at the cottage on the weekend. Janet laughs, pats her hair. "Sure, why not?" she replies, and adds that she's been offered a job in the cosmetics section of a department store. She starts in two weeks and needs to shop for decent clothes, make-up. She *plans to have her hair done like this, she says, and thrusts a magazine at Sophie. The woman in the magazine has smooth blonde hair piled high on her head. She is smiling, showing hard, white teeth.*

On Saturday afternoon, Janet borrows Betty's car and drives to the cottage with Sophie. The front door is locked. The back door gapes open.

Sophie checks each room, each closet and cupboard. She opens the fridge and pulls out a plate holding a slice of chocolate cake.

Janet phones her family, checks with neighbours and calls the police. Sophie sits on the doorstep until the sun drops behind the trees.

Day after day, frogmen slide into the water, emerge dripping, glisten in the sun like alien beings. They sit on the dock between dives and drink soft drinks from cans. They bring up a grey raincoat with a tear on the right sleeve, then a faded pink running shoe, a tartan scarf and a long-sleeved check shirt with black stains. Janet shakes her head each time.

"That's it," she says when they bring up a worn brown shoe late one afternoon. She turns it over. "That hole—he never had it fixed. That's it."

The police express regrets but, after six days, feel that continuing the search would be futile.

Janet builds a bonfire when they leave. She drags out Stefan's books, clothes, photographs, and hurls them onto the flames. Sophie snatches the photograph of her father from the living room wall and hides it in her closet, behind her boots. She watches Janet from the back door. She grips the door frame so hard her fingers hurt. Flames snap and spit. Janet flickers dark and light as she raises her arms and lifts her face to the sky, as if she is dancing.

I'll never forgive you, Sophie screams in her head. Never, never, never.

One year later, Janet marries Bill, a red-faced widower with a pink scalp, her boss at the store. She wears a dress of multiple layers of thin, pale blue fabric at her wedding. There are small white daisies in her hair. Bill slips an arm around Janet's shoulders at the reception. She smiles into his face as she raises a glass of champagne.

"The past is past," she announces.

—

Bill and Janet live in a long white bungalow in a neighbourhood where streets are straight, lawns carpet-green. Clusters of pink and white begonias pack the flower beds beneath the front windows of their house.

The walls inside are papered or painted with colours Janet calls citron, robin's egg blue, dusty rose. Silk roses, lilies, orchids fill each corner. There's a persistent sharp scent throughout the house which, Sophie has discovered, emanates from the pretend lemons stuck in what look like egg cups hidden behind curtains, in drawers and closets. There is no mould, no rot, no dust, not one dark corner anywhere.

Every year, when Sophie arrives for the birthday, Bill and Janet pick her up at the airport. Janet insists Sophie sit in the front, beside Bill. She spreads herself in the back. She leans forward, taps Sophie's shoulder as she talks. When they reach the road that runs parallel to the river, Sophie forces herself to concentrate on Janet's voice, the tap tap of Janet's finger on her shoulder. The sun pushes through the window and she blinks. She tries to focus straight ahead, to ignore patches of water that sparkle between buildings and trees.

But she cannot stop herself from turning, and she can't stop the tape that is always activated in her head. The old cottage is almost an hour's drive away, but who knows? *Maybe over there. Or over here.* A face wavers in the side window. Dark hair, dark eyes that glisten like glass. Skin so white it could be bone. She hears the croak of a frog. The night rustle of leaves. Low, slow words. *There's no difference between the past and the present when the past is still going on in your head.*

"Lovely," Janet murmurs when Sophie presents the gift. Her red-tipped fingers slide over the bow, smooth the paper over and over. "Almost too pretty to open." Disappointment seeps from her voice, but she undoes the wrapping and turns to the window.

The sun slides through the glass and trickles through Janet's hair which she now keeps rusty red, the colour of a pomegranate. She removes the wrapping, tilts the painting this way and that, lowers it and stares at Sophie as if she is looking for something, the small child, perhaps, who once scribbled ducks, a sun with wriggly rays, giant red and orange flowers, and people with lips turned up at the sides. Sophie stares back. Janet's hands tremble. Flakes of powder are trapped in the folds of her skin. Her mouth creases into a pleat as she forces some approving sound from her lips.

And Sophie remembers the woman with wild, pale curls, the smooth pink skin. Broad feet stomping through the vegetable garden. Firm hands plucking tomatoes and beans, yanking carrots. And suddenly she wants to place her fingers on Janet's arm. She wants to see Janet smile with pleasure and surprise. But she cannot make herself move. She is frozen, and the moment is lost.

At the birthday barbecue each year there are neighbours, friends old and new, Bill's and Janet's family. And the spare man, sometimes two. The spare man had a flat stomach once, a head of thick hair, and he talked with confidence, arrogance, about his ambitions, plans for his life. He parked a low, sleek car as close to the house as possible.

Now he is grey, balding, and his stomach is soft. Divorced—or sometimes widowed—he is eager to meet Janet's daughter, the artist, who's doing so well on the west coast. When Sophie extends her hand, he holds it too long in his damp palm.

Sophie smiles, excuses herself, brings out salads, pours soft drinks for the children. She slips from person to person, allocates each a portion of her time. Whenever she turns briefly to the spare man, Janet is there, in the corner of her eye, watching.

Dusk sweeps the garden. The children are querulous, their voices high, unreal. The adults, lethargic from too much food and drink, sink like soft dolls into the garden chairs.

Sophie scoops up dishes and glasses.

"Stop," Janet shouts with mock-horror. "Relax, have fun."

Sophie shakes her head, carries on. The guests smile and Sophie sees herself through their eyes. She is the good daughter, home for her mother's birthday, in her mother's garden, among family and her mother's friends. Everyone in the world is somewhere.

And some people are in two places at once. *She is here* and she is *there* on the dock, bare feet skimming the cool water. The river breeze tickles her skin. There's the roar of a lone motor boat, the slap slap of water against the dock. Silence. A sideways glance of the moon on black water. The clink of a bottle. A low, soft splash.

"Did you have a good time?" Janet asks when the guests have left.

"Very nice," Sophie replies.

"Did you like anyone in particular?" Janet drags out plastic wrap as she speaks, stretches it over salads and cold cuts with intense concentration.

"Everyone was very nice."

"Friends and family. Aren't they wonderful?" Janet persists. "You're so far away," she adds, when Sophie doesn't reply. "But you're happy out there, are you?"

Sophie nods, scrapes leftovers into the garbage. Some day she will tell Janet something that will alarm her. She will tell her that it's not happiness she feels, exactly. She's more relieved than happy, which is a kind of happiness, in a way. When she opens her eyes on a day that is too bright, she is relieved to find herself alone so she can close her eyes again until the light is less intense. When she picks up a newspaper and reads about a baby found in a trash can, a car accident that destroyed a mother and father but left the child unharmed, or an article about a son who has been lost in a war he knew nothing about, she is relieved that she can crumple the paper and throw it away.

Alone, she can flick the switch on the radio, change the channel on the TV. She can tread carefully, one deliberate step after another. She can look down to avoid holes, soft spots she may sink into. Relief, she figures, is far more important than love. It allows you to sleep at night.

—

Sophie checks her wallet, her ticket again and stretches out on the bed. There are stars in the skylight tonight. Although she is not aware of being nervous, she wakes often the night before she flies, and when she does sleep, she always dreams the same dream. A plane somersaults in the sky. People tumble out, limbs spread. Magazines, dishes, plummet to earth. Suitcases spill open. Shirts, pants, dresses, flap like sails. And tonight there will be bones. She is sure of this. Long white bones, gleaming as if polished. Small bones that clink in the void.

Her flight is at ten. She sets her alarm for five. The shapes have almost come together in her head and the outline will be ready before she leaves. Bones so luminous against the blackness, they hardly bear looking at. A skull, but not immediately recognizable as one. Positioned somewhere in the shadows, curtained by a cloud or a trickle of water thin as a silk scarf, to the left—or maybe to the right—of the canvas. Certainly not in the centre where a skull would be too obvious, too easy to dismiss as a gimmick, a cheap trick. And at the bottom, a small, distorted figure trapped in the moon's icy light, arms extended, palms up.

SATURDAY

"Do you need groceries?" Brian says into the phone. "Milk? Bread?" He takes a sip of coffee, glances at Clare. She is sitting at the kitchen table with her back to him, holding her coffee cup with both hands. Her head is bent, exposing a triangle of pale skin on the back of her neck.

"All right. Tell Rachel I'll pick her up in twenty minutes." Brian replaces the phone. "Mary sounds really sick," he says to Clare. "Full of a cold."

Clare peers into her cup. "This isn't your Saturday."

"I know it isn't." Brian holds back the edge from his voice. "But Mary is sick," he repeats carefully. "We can do the chores next weekend just as well."

He pats the back pocket of his jeans where he'd stuffed the list Clare gave him last night. She had made two lists, one for each of them, of chores that must be done this Saturday, tedious things they've been putting off for weeks, months. She'd written the most important chores at the top and emphasized them with an asterisk. *Replace cracked basement window, fix bathroom tap, fix wheel on Edward's stroller.* These items head Brian's list.

As Brian laces his running shoes and removes his car keys from the hook on the wall, he remembers that Clare's mother is supposed to pick up Edward later this morning and take him home with her to keep him out of the way. He hangs about in the doorway for a moment, wondering if he should say something, apologize perhaps. The thought irritates him and he's about to turn away when Edward runs into the room, his TV cartoons abandoned. The child's feet are bare, his hair is still tangled from sleep.

Brian picks him up, raises him over his head. "I'm off to get Rachel, all right? Okay?"

"Okay," Edward shouts. "Okay."

Brian hugs him and turns to Clare to draw her into the circle. She looks up, smiles faintly.

"Well. I'm off. We'll do the chores next weekend. Promise. You'd better call your mother and explain." Brian removes Edward's fingers from around his neck and deposits the child on the floor. "I'm sorry, Clare."

"It's all right." She hesitates. "I've half-asked the Johnsons for dinner next Saturday but I'm sure they'll forgive me if I cancel. There won't be time to cook and do the chores."

Brian's hand hovers over the doorknob.

"Don't worry about it," she adds. "It's nothing." She's smiling properly now as she rises, scoops up the cups and plates from the table and begins to stack them in the dishwasher.

—

Rachel has turned her face towards the car window and Brian must pretend that he doesn't know she's sucking her thumb behind the long pale hair she's made into a curtain to cover one side of her face. Once, last summer, he'd told her that a child of eight was too old for a habit like this and she'd turned away and disappeared through the back door, into the garden. She returned an hour later with puffy, reddened eyes and shook her head when Brian asked if she'd like to come to the mall with him, something she usually likes to do.

Brian was in such a hurry today he forgot to retrieve the big yellow laundry basket containing Rachel's belongings—toys and books that he has bought for her and a few items of clothing—from the cupboard in the family room. He usually brings the basket up to the spare bedroom before he picks her up, and leaves it there on the floor for her to unpack. The books go on the bottom shelf of the small bookcase, in order of size. The porcelain dolls that Rachel collects, and which Brian buys for her when he needs to see her smile, are arranged on the dresser, their rigid limbs extended, narrow feet peering out from beneath stiff skirts. The soft toys are propped up on the bed against the wall, so that Rachel can reach out for the one she wants when she is in bed.

When Rachel leaves, Clare packs these items into the laundry basket again and takes them back downstairs. There are so many toys and books wedged into the basket now, they spill over the top while she is carrying them, and a book or a toy often clatters to the floor. It's only a matter of time, Brian has warned Clare, before something gets broken. Rachel will be very upset. The spare room should be kept uncluttered, ready for guests, Clare replied. She spoke slowly, as if she were explaining something to a child, and Brian had to leave the room to keep himself from shouting that not once in their five years of married life have they ever had an overnight guest.

"Here we are," Brian says.

Rachel tucks her hair behind her ears. The gesture is Mary's, and when Rachel turns towards Brian he realizes that even her eyes are her mother's, that strange colour that is sometimes green, sometimes grey.

The other day, when he and Clare were at the mall, they saw Rachel and Mary coming out of the book store. Clare stood still, watching mother and daughter head for the exit.

"She looks just like her mother," she said. Her voice was taut, cold, as if she were describing an imperfection and Brian, who had raised his arm and was about to call out Mary's and Rachel's names, stopped and stared at his wife.

"Come on." She tugged his arm. "We have shopping to do."

"She's my daughter," Brian said. You're a mother, he wanted to add. You should understand. But Clare was already walking, almost running ahead.

Edward is framed in the living room window, his arms extended. Rachel squints into the sun. "Hi, Eddie," she calls.

"Don't let Clare hear you call him that."

"Sometimes I forget. Besides, it's a silly name."

Brian glances sideways at her. Her face is bland but he wonders if he should ever have told her that the name was Clare's choice. He had laughed and shaken his head at the time. I can live with it, he'd said, but now he remembers Rachel's small face turned up towards him, her eyes bright, absorbed, her lips drawn in as if she had bitten off a smile.

"Hello, Rachel." Clare holds the door open. "How nice to see you," she says.

She stands back, smiling as they enter. Edward runs to his mother and in a brief moment of shyness, clings to her leg. Clare's fingers graze the top of his head. "Why don't you show Rachel your new play-dough?" she asks. "It's on the shelf, in the kitchen."

Brian follows Rachel inside. Clare ushers everyone around the kitchen table. The room is drenched with sunshine. Such a beautiful day shouldn't be wasted, Clare insists, glancing through the window. Her voice is even and smooth. Brian watches her.

Sometimes there are moments that surprise him: small, hopeful stars that break out unexpectedly and lift him inside. These moments are numbered and hoarded in his mind, snapshots that he needs to take out and inspect from time to time. There was that glittering day last winter when he'd heard voices outside and had put aside the papers he'd been working on to look out of the window. Clare was striding towards the snowman Rachel had made for Edward in the front garden. She was carrying Brian's purple ski hat and his torn blue scarf; she slipped the hat over the snowman's head, wound the scarf around his neck. She pulled a pair of sunglasses from her pocket and stuck them over the snowman's carrot nose and the three of them joined hands and skipped around the snowman, singing and laughing. Then Clare broke away and swept up Edward in a brief hug. She released him and turned quickly, to hug Rachel. She was smiling, her face flushed with winter's sharpness.

Then, again, last Sunday afternoon when Edward was having his nap, Brian poked his head into the kitchen to find a clutter of dishes, spoons and empty eggshells scattered over the counters and the table. The floor, every surface, seemed to be covered with a thin dusting of flour, like a first snowfall. Rachel was pouring blueberries into a big white bowl that Clare was holding in her arms. They both looked up and smiled at him with blue-stained lips. He watched them briefly, without speaking, and retreated, closing the door softly behind him.

"I can take Edward to the park," Rachel offers.

"The beach would be better," Clare replies. "If we leave now, we'll beat the crowds."

Rachel looks around. "What about the museum? No one else will be there so it won't be crowded and it's air-conditioned so we'll stay cool. We'll probably have the whole place to ourselves."

"Well," Brian nods, "that makes sense."

"Perhaps." Clare speaks slowly. She frowns, as if she's thinking hard. "But you must remember, Rachel, that Edward loves the beach. Your father and I enjoy it, too. Young children don't find museums very interesting." She pats Rachel's hand. "You must try to be more considerate. Think of others sometimes."

Rachel reddens and looks down at her hands.

"Dinosaurs. I want to see dinosaurs." Edward slides from his chair. He tugs his mother's arm.

Rachel lifts her chin, her face still hot, pink. "Edward likes the museum. He wants to go."

"If the kids want to go to the museum, then for heaven's sake, let them go." Brian's voice is sharp and Clare's lips tighten. "Why don't you stay home, Clare?" he adds quickly. "You need time to yourself. I'll take them out for lunch and we'll be back in time for Edward's nap."

Edward tugs Clare's arm again. She frees herself from him and spreads her arms in a gesture of mock defeat. Brian pulls Edward onto his lap and looks over his son's head at Rachel. She grins at him. From the corner of his eye Brian can see that Clare has observed this exchange.

"Come on, old man." He turns to his son. "Go bring your running shoes."

Edward disappears and returns quickly with his shoes. Brian kneels on the floor to help him put them on. Rachel inspects Edward's painting on the fridge door while she waits; there's a sun the size and colour of an egg yolk in the middle of the large white sheet and a row of red and yellow flowers along the bottom, their colours mingling, running into one another.

"He's pretty good, isn't he?" Rachel addresses Clare. "And he isn't even three yet."

Clare has picked up a pencil and paper and is jotting down items, one beneath the other, as if she's making a shopping list. She doesn't look up. Rachel's hand lingers over her mouth. She traces her upper lip with her forefinger, presses and pulls away. Brian glances at her quickly as he struggles with a knot in Edward's shoelace.

Last week, Mary told Brian that one of the children at school had pointed out to Rachel that her upper front teeth are weird. Rabbit-face, the child had taunted and Rachel cried into her dinner and again in bed that night. There's no point in braces, Mary added, until she stops sucking her thumb. Brian is sure Rachel had stopped once, when she was still a toddler. It seems important these days to remember when she started again, but he doesn't want Rachel to know of his concern. He doesn't want her to realize that he watches her when she prods her lips and touches her teeth tentatively. Somehow it seems to him that she's probing a wound that she cannot leave alone.

"Does it bother you, Rachel?" Clare looks at Rachel, tilts her head to one side.

"What?"

"The little problem with your teeth. It's such a shame. You're a pretty girl, really."

"Not now, Clare," Brian says quietly.

He tries to think of something to say that will distract Rachel but she has already turned and run out of the room.

—

Brian settles Edward in his car seat in the back of the car and climbs into the front. He slips his seat belt across his shoulder, clicks it into place.

"All right?" he turns to Rachel. She nods.

Clare steps into the garden, carrying a paper bag. She snaps the dead-heads from the cluster of pink and red impatiens beside the front door and drops them into the bag. Edward taps on the car window and yells good-bye. Clare straightens, waves and turns to the flowers again.

The other evening when they were sitting in the family room, reading, Clare lowered her book and began to talk about having another child. Edward should have a companion so that he doesn't grow up spoiled, she said. It would be nice to have a little girl. Her mild, reasonable voice spread across the room and Brian rose, crossed the floor abruptly, leaned over her and gripped her arms hard.

"We already have a girl," he snapped into her white face. "Haven't you noticed?"

"Brian," she whispered.

"Sorry," he said and released her.

He watched livid red marks replace the pale imprints of his hands on Clare's bare arms. She rubbed them and said it didn't matter. They have never spoken of the incident but Brian thinks about it from time to time. He remembers the way they padded softly through the house for days afterwards, the way they spoke quietly and slowly, as if a sudden noise or movement would shatter something in the room.

Edward taps on the window again and calls to his mother. She drops the paper bag at her feet and, smiling, holds both arms high to wave an exaggerated wave. In her shorts and white T-shirt, her feet in socks and running shoes, she seems young, fragile, almost a child herself. Brian softens. He raises his arm and smiles in her direction as he backs out of the driveway.

—

Clare is reading the papers when they return. She folds the section she has in her hands when she sees them, places it carefully on the pile of papers beside her feet. The children run out the back door, slamming it behind them. Brian stands by the window, watching them racing around the garden.

"They're having fun."

"You were much longer than I expected. Edward hasn't had his nap."

"He'll be all right. We had lunch and then they wanted to go to the park so we bought bread and fed the ducks. I think I'll make a start on that window."

The basement window is cloudy, with a layer of dust inside, spattered with water and dirt on the outside. Brian runs the tips of his fingers along the crack and rubs a circle in the corner to clear away the dust. Rachel and

Edward are caught up in the circle he has made in the glass. They are standing beneath the apple tree at the bottom of the garden. Rachel is leaning over Edward; their heads are almost touching. Rachel straightens suddenly and Edward steps back and raises his arms while she struggles to lift him. They start laughing and collapse on the ground. They rise and try again. Edward grabs the lowest branch of the tree with one hand and tries to pull himself up while Rachel pushes from beneath. He hooks a leg over the branch, clutches it with his hands and manages to pull himself up. He stands, remains poised for a moment as he reaches for the tree trunk with one hand, then overbalances suddenly and tumbles to the ground.

Brian races upstairs. By the time he has reached the back door, Clare is already running across the lawn, scattering papers over the grass. Edward is crying, a small, jagged sound that turns into a shriek when Clare reaches him and picks him up. Blood trickles from his nose. He leans his head briefly against his mother's arm and when he removes it, there's a crimson stain on her white sleeve.

"It's just a nose bleed." Rachel's face is pale. "He'll be okay."

"What was he doing in the tree? He could have been killed."

"He just bumped his nose."

"You don't give a damn, do you? Do you?"

Rachel steps back and presses herself against the tree. Clare deposits Edward on the grass and begins to move towards her. Brian is immobile in the doorway. She's going to hit her, he is thinking. She's going to hurt her. He can't move, can't call out. Clare raises her arm and Rachel breaks away from the tree and runs past her, screaming, across the lawn towards her father.

Clare turns, faces Brian. Silence descends on the garden. A dog barks somewhere. Brian takes Rachel's hand and walks quickly across the garden, through the side gate to the car. Edward wriggles away from Clare and runs after them. He rattles the closed gate and screams for his father.

—

When Brian and Rachel return, there's a green salad in a large glass bowl and a platter of steaks and hamburgers on the kitchen table. Clare is scrubbing potatoes at the sink. She has changed into a dress covered with large red and purple flowers and blue-green leaves in the shape of hearts. Edward is up from his nap, she tells them, glancing over her shoulder, and is playing in the family room. His nose, by the way, is fine. She pierces the potatoes with a fork, arranges them in the microwave, then moves quickly around the kitchen, opening drawers and cupboards, taking out plates, cutlery, salt and pepper.

"Clare." Brian touches her arm as she passes. He'd taken Rachel to a movie after the garden incident but he can't remember which one. He kept seeing Rachel's white face in the dark, Clare moving towards her.

"I'm starving, aren't you?" Clare removes a glass dish from the refrigerator and brings it to Rachel. "Look what Edward and I made. Your favourite dessert—chocolate mousse with orange. Such sophisticated taste. Edward thinks it's chocolate pudding, the kind you make out of a packet." She smiles. "The Philistine."

Brian looks at Rachel; he raises his eyebrows.

"Thank you," she says.

When she leaves the room, Brian touches Clare's arm again. "Clare, we should talk."

"Yes, I'm sorry about that business earlier. I can't believe I got so upset. I was just worried about Edward." She picks up the cutlery and begins to set the table. She pauses, holding a fork in her hand. "Really, Brian, I am sorry. Would you look after the meat?"

Brian stares at the platter. Two T-bones. Two large hamburgers: one for Edward, one for Rachel. The meat is too bright, too red against the glossy whiteness of the dish. He picks up the platter and steps outside.

Rachel and Edward are framed in the family room window, sitting on the floor in the darkened room, their faces ghostly in the television's flickering light. Brian sees the back of Clare's dark head through the glass kitchen door, the flowers splattered over her dress, the table set for four with the salad bowl in the centre.

He places the platter on the patio table, lights the barbecue and lowers himself into a chair. The sky is on fire, the evening golden. His limbs are bronzed, unreal, the limbs of a statue or some mythical being. He reaches for the platter and the tips of his fingers slide into the blood that has seeped from the meat and accumulated around the edges. He withdraws his hands quickly and stares at them.

Rachel and Edward have moved to the family room window; they are jostling each other with their elbows, pushing their faces and the palms of their hands hard against the glass. Their flattened, distorted features are grotesque. Brian turns his face away. He sits very still in the darkening garden, his back pressed hard against the seat, the palms of his hands flat, rigid on his thighs.

NEST

When the cottage has been cleaned and the boxes and suitcases unpacked, Diane looks around for empty jars so the children can go to the water's edge to hunt for tadpoles among the reeds. She throws the wet cleaning cloths into a bucket and carries them out to hang on the line. Tom is standing beneath the maple, staring up at a nest in the crook of the lowest branch. A robin emerges, flutters between the leaves and disappears over the lake.

"The baby bird fell out again," Tom says as Diane walks by.

Early this morning soon after they arrived to open the cottage for the season, Diane made coffee and carried out two mugs on a tray. Tom dragged the old lawn mower from the shed and surveyed the dandelions sprinkled like bright stars through the long grass. He sank to his knees in front of the machine, poked a finger into a rusty spot on the metal, peered at it.

"It'll be a miracle if this thing still works," he muttered. He turned away suddenly and scooped something from a clump of grass. He held up his cupped hand. "A tiny bird," he said. He rose slowly and called to the children.

Emma and Sarah came running and pried his fingers open.

"Oh, it's ugly," they said. "Is it really a bird? Poor thing. Poor little bird. Will it get feathers soon, Dad?"

"Sure it will."

Diane glanced at the lake shore. "Where did Matthew go?" she asked. The girls shrugged. "Tom? Have you seen him?"

"I'll go find him in a minute."

"Dad, will the baby bird be all right?"

"I think so. I'll put it back." Tom turned towards Diane. "Come have a look, Diane." He extended his arm towards her and spread his fingers open.

Diane has seen pictures of newly-hatched birds. They are hairless and their skin is puckered like an old bag that is too big to hold their bones. Their heads are huge, their eyes too round, too bright. Their beaks are always open. She turned her head slightly and glanced at the creature in Tom's hand.

"It doesn't look much like a bird," she said.

"Let me see. Let me see." Matthew hurtled towards them from behind the cottage. He ran and jumped; he held his arms high above his head and his watch glistened, flashed briefly in the sun.

"Be careful! Be careful!" The girls grabbed the back of Matthew's T-shirt as he reached for Tom's hand. "Don't hurt it."

"From here, he looks like a normal kid," Diane whispered when Tom had returned the bird to the nest and the children were walking away. She pressed both hands around her coffee mug to keep them from trembling.

"That's not fair, Diane."

"No, I know. I'm sorry. I didn't mean it."

Tom is still staring up at the tree. "I don't understand it. That nest is so sturdy, the sides so high. How does it happen?"

"Survival of the fittest," she replies, softly.

"He really does seem to be getting better," Tom says, later. He is staring through the screen at Matthew who is turning the picnic table into a fort with old blankets and pieces of wood. "He's quieter. Sleeps longer. Doesn't do quite so many dumb things. He's even beginning to understand that there's a connection between action and consequence."

Tom rises, steps up behind Diane, touches her shoulders, coaxing her into their old game of pretending that Matthew is harmless, a clown. "Remember last summer when he painted a white stripe on Mrs. Johnson's black mutt?"

Diane turns sharply. "And the time he backed the car out of the driveway and almost killed our neighbour?"

Tom's face is moist. The puffy skin beneath his eyes has a violet tinge. "Look, Diane, he's hyperactive, not crazy. He can't help it."

"I know that."

"He'll get better. He's only eight. Give him time."

"They keep calling me to the school. I feel as if I'm on duty all the time."

"It won't last. He is getting better. Can't you see?"

"All the neighbours and even his teachers think there must be more to this problem of his. They think we're hiding something, doing something wrong. Last time I was called to the school to bring him home the principal wouldn't look at me. He wouldn't even say hello." Diane touches Tom's arm. "What will happen to him, Tom? He won't be a child forever."

Tom grabs the bag of charcoal from behind the door. Diane sits down heavily on the nearest chair. She listens to Tom's feet pounding down the wooden steps. In the kitchen the girls are removing food from the fridge and setting the table. The clink of plates, the shuffle of bare feet across the wooden floor, their murmurs, fill the spaces in the cottage. The slanting rays of the late afternoon light slide in and stretch across the room. Diane closes her eyes and lifts her face towards them.

After dinner, the girls spread themselves outside on the grass, displaying thin, white winter limbs in the softening light. They have painted their fingernails bright red, like chunks of hard, smooth candy and have set each other's long hair in the massive pink rollers that were stuffed in the bottom of the bathroom cupboard. They look comical, top-heavy, like overgrown Kewpies. They have arranged bottles of purple, red and pink nail polish and an assortment of lipsticks and eyeshadows two by two on a folded towel.

When Matthew is ordered to come inside he grabs an apple from the fridge and collapses on the couch beside Diane. He opens a comic book and begins to flip through the pages. Diane stares at the back of his bent head. His neck is thin and fragile and pale at the line just beneath his hair where the sun could not reach. She imagines touching him, drawing him towards her, holding him for a moment. His mandatory quiet times had once been only a minute here and there throughout the day but now they stretch to five minutes, and sometimes even more. Perhaps, she thinks, as something lifts inside her, perhaps Tom is right.

A car door slams outside. Matthew throws the apple across the floor, jumps up and disappears, leaving the door swinging behind him. Diane watches him through the window as he runs across the grass, shouting, kicking his sisters' make-up.

"Mom!" Sarah screams. She marches towards the cottage.

"I know. I know." Diane rushes out.

Janet Brown is waving from next door. Her husband, Jim, and their son Andrew, are struggling from the car with knapsacks and suitcases.

Diane waves back enthusiastically. Last year, when the Browns closed up for winter, they didn't even say good-bye. The day before, Matthew had led the younger Andrew on what he called a secret expedition. The boys left after breakfast and when they hadn't returned by late afternoon, a group of cottagers was organized to search for them. It was almost dark when they were found, more than two miles away. They were hungry and tired and covered with mosquito bites. Andrew began to cry when he saw his parents. Matthew was hanging from a nearby tree. He was waving, calling to the rescuers, laughing.

"He doesn't even know what he's done, does he?" Janet turned to Diane, her mouth twisted. Her face rose ghostlike in the dusk, accusing. God, Diane thought. Oh, God.

Matthew has reached the Browns' car, begins to drag out bags and boxes and scatters them over the ground.

"Hang on there," Jim tells him. "Hang on."

"Matthew." Tom's voice stretches across the two properties. "I need your help over here. Right now."

—

The sound of crying wakes Diane in the middle of the night. She's confused for a moment and imagines it's one of the children, crying to be fed. When she becomes fully conscious, she realizes it's a thinner, more desperate sound than her children ever made and she knows that it's the bird, fallen out of its nest again. She turns to Tom who is breathing deeply, steadily beside her.

The slice of moon from the uncurtained window has lit up Tom's face and turned it blue-grey, the colour of stone. Tom always falls asleep quickly and is never wakened by noises—police sirens, dogs barking, cat fights beneath the window—that easily pierce Diane's fragile nighttime state. He teases her over the breakfast table sometimes as she reaches again and again for the coffee pot. Tom claims he sleeps the sleep of the innocent, deep and dreamless, the sleep of a child. Diane has always believed he was joking, poking gentle fun to lighten her mood. Now, lying with her eyes open, staring at dark shapes on the walls and ceiling, she thinks of the possibility that he isn't joking, that he believes she is guilty of something, of lacking faith, perhaps, or even love, and has chosen to accuse her in this way. She raises her hand to touch his shoulder, to wake him, and imagines hitting him hard, so she rolls over quickly and turns her back on him. She slips her hands beneath her cheek to keep them still, anchored.

She grows stiff with the effort of trying to get back to sleep. The luminous hands of the clock shift. Half an hour and shrill cries still punctuate the darkness. One hour. Two. The wind picks up, races through the trees and she pulls the covers over her ears. Raindrops begin a soft patter on the roof. The cries grow faint, stop as the sky turns silver and, in two minutes, she is fast asleep.

Emma brings the dead bird into the cottage after breakfast and holds it out mutely to her father.

Tom takes Emma's hand in both his and inspects the bird. "Damn." He shakes his head.

"Sarah and I are going to bury it."

The girls wrap the bird in a tissue and place it reverently inside an empty yogurt container. They go outside and prod the ground with sticks, looking for a suitable burial spot.

"Cool this morning." Tom sniffs the air through the screen, his back to Diane. "Poor devil didn't stand a chance."

Tom and Diane watch the funeral preparations from the porch, the cross fashioned from twigs and a piece of string taking shape in Emma's hands. Sarah sits on the grass, her lap strewn with dandelions and Queen Anne's lace. She knots the stems together, twists them into wreaths and bouquets. Jim Brown is packing fishing rods and a cooler into his motor boat. Andrew passes him three orange lifejackets. Jim has promised to take Andrew and Matthew to the island in the middle of the lake for a couple of hours this morning to fish. Matthew runs back and forth on the dock, hopping from one foot to another, calling Andrew's name.

"He'll be all right," Tom says.

"Will he?" Diane's voice is tight.

"I mean now, today," he replies sharply. "Jim will keep him busy. It'll tire him out."

"Oh, Tom." They turn towards each other, their hands raised, fingers about to touch.

"Darn." Tom indicates Matthew with a shake of his head. The boy has climbed into the boat and is slipping a lifejacket over his pale blue T-shirt. "He'll be cold out there on the lake." Tom grabs a sweater and in a minute he's out of the cottage, running towards the motor boat, calling Matthew, waving the sweater in the air.

Diane returns to the kitchen, scoops up the breakfast dishes and carries them to the sink. She turns on the tap and stands for a long time, watching the water running over her hands, trickling between her fingers.

—

Later, she drags a chair to the edge of the lake and sits with a book on her lap. The funeral has been completed and a crooked cross protrudes from the mound of earth and flowers beneath the maple. The girls are out on the lake in the canoe. Emma paddles slowly. Sarah leans back, her hands trailing over the sides, her fingers skimming the water. Tom stands on the dock, looking out. The clouds are small and high, the lake glints like a sheet of glass.

Tom raises his hand over his eyes. "They're coming back," he says.

The clatter of a starting motor fills the air. The boat shifts away from the island, picks up speed. It parts the surface of the water, turns to avoid a large rock and tips slightly, gracefully, to one side.

Tom turns to Diane. "Someone's climbing over the seats."

Diane pulls herself forward and squints into the sun. She can see a slender figure in a blue T-shirt, a pair of white shorts. "Matthew," she says. "He's not wearing his lifejacket." The book slides from her lap.

"Jim hasn't seen him." Tom cups his hands around his mouth. "Jim!" he calls. "Jim!"

The boy remains poised on the side of the boat for one second. Then he leans over suddenly and plunges into the water.

Janet Brown runs from her cottage. "For heaven's sake! The lake is still freezing." She waves both arms at Jim but he has already stopped the boat and is standing up, looking around. They are all silent, waiting, watching the water ripple and shimmer, listening to its slap, slap against the dock. Tom calls to Emma and Sarah, urging them to paddle towards the boat. The girls turn the canoe around. Matthew's head appears from behind the large rock.

"Fooled you," he shouts. "Fooled you all!"

His voice splinters in the air. He swims towards the boat and Jim leans over and hauls him in by the back of the neck. Matthew stands with his head down, his arms crossed over his chest and Jim slips out of his own sweater and throws it over him.

Diane reaches for her book, opens it, arranges it carefully on her lap. She smooths the pages over and over with the palms of her hands. Tom is saying something about a warm shower and clean, dry clothes. His voice is blurred, as if it is coming from far away. Diane can feel his eyes on her as she sits, her shoulders rounded, curved in defeat, trying to make sense of the words that keep shifting, fluttering, on the page.

THE MANGO TREE

Early that year, before I was aware of the cracks that would soon appear in our lives, I waited for the rains the way I had always done, so I could catch the frogs and tadpoles that sprouted in our flooded field. But the rains were late and I was afraid they wouldn't come at all. The fields were as dry and dusty as old parchment, the sky too blue. Every day, I looked for signs that would usher in the first storm: the sudden rustle of leaves; the long, yellowed grasses bending, running in waves beneath a charcoal sky; air that shimmered like glass over parched fields, making the distant white buildings of Nairobi tremble, as if they were underwater.

During the rainy season, as long as I could remember, the children in our area converged daily in the field at the bottom of the slope behind our house. Soon after the rains began, the field turned into a large murky pond. Knee-deep in water, bare feet sinking in the mud, we waded in, waving butterfly nets, laughing, ready to slap the nets down at the sight of a small, darting creature. We used the frogs for races or traded them as if they were stamps or bubble gum cards. The smallest frogs, not much bigger than a thumbnail, were prized above all others because of their speed and their smooth, exquisite skin—the colour of a green apple. They were lined up in the mud at the edge of the water and prodded with sharpened sticks so they would jump towards the finishing line, a row of stones we had laid out. There was much laughter, shouting and shoving during each race, and in the confusion someone always prodded a small soft body too hard and impaled it. I barely touched the frogs with my stick. I knew they did just as well if they were not frightened. But the other children were scornful and I began to wonder if I was lacking something—courage, perhaps.

I crossed my fingers. Please God, I prayed, if you make it rain I promise I'll never tease Stephen again. This was my favourite prayer, the one I used most often in my requests. I would forget the promise later, whether the request was granted or not, until the next time. But God was forgiving that year.

If my prayers and entreaties had been denied, what then? What would have happened? Or not happened? Mrs. Cox, our teacher, claimed that everything that happened in each person's life was recorded in some mysterious way, as if by some massive, supernatural camera. On Judgement Day it was played back, like a reel of a film, for everyone to see.

What about the future? I wanted to know. Was it all there on the film already and was I—and everyone else—just playing parts like actors in a script that had already been written? And, if so, could I snip off the parts I didn't like and change them? Mrs. Cox flapped her hand when I asked these questions, as if they were not worthy of a response.

Then, one afternoon, I knew the rains would come. A dark line of birds was poised over the dried fields. The sky was a pale blue sheet, smooth as an eggshell, but I could smell something—a distant dampness— as I walked towards the stables. I was clutching a handful of jars for the frogs and tadpoles I intended to catch. Because I was not permitted to play in the field when it flooded, in what my parents called *that filthy water*, I kept the jars in the loft above the stables. Joseph always placed bundles of hay near the entrance so that if my father popped his head up casually from below—as he sometimes did—he wouldn't see them. Joseph would pierce holes in the lids of my jars and later, I would fill each one with the choicest leaves I could find and sprinkle them with water. I wasn't sure what frogs liked to eat but I always threw in a few dead ants and flies, as well.

I passed a chameleon who was staring at me from one of the lower branches of the old mango tree. I reached for it but it disappeared with a smart flick of its tail. I had seen a snake in that tree, once, wrapped around the trunk. It was like a picture in our classroom: a serpent coiled around a tree; Adam and Eve standing beneath it, clutching huge leaves in front of their naked bodies. Mrs. Cox *explained* the picture, explained how Adam and Eve were perfectly happy and unaware of evil until they plucked an apple from the forbidden Tree. I turned to Klara as Mrs. Cox was speaking and I rolled my eyes.

Klara and her parents were DPs and lived in the camp across the river, set up by people like us, out of kindness, after the war. Whenever we drove into Nairobi, we could see the square, drab houses of the camp huddled together, their corrugated metal roofs glinting in the sun. Mother said I must not be too friendly with Klara, but I must always be polite. I hung around Klara, anyway; it seemed to me that she knew everything. And she could punch any boy who called her a dirty DP, with a fist as hard and bony as a rock.

Load of rubbish, I said to Klara later, after Mrs. Cox's comments on Adam and Eve. How can evil exist if people are not aware of it? Good and evil are pretty straightforward. Lying, stealing, are evil. Telling the truth is good, especially if you are scared. When I give a shilling to one of those beggars in Nairobi, that's especially good, isn't it?

Why? Klara asked. She was wearing an old dress of mine that my mother had ordered me to throw out because the seams were loose. Klara had sewn up the seams and added a round, crocheted collar and the dress looked fine, although it hung loosely on her much thinner frame. Why? she asked again.

Because looking at those cloudy eyes or those stumps wrapped in filthy rags is revolting, I replied. And they stink. It makes my stomach turn.

I wonder how the beggars' stomachs feel, Klara said. What do you think?

As I reached the stable door, Wambui stepped out and began to run along the path. She passed me swiftly, her head lowered, dodging the sharp pebbles on the path as skillfully as a dancer, with her small, bare feet. "*Jambo!*" I called but she disappeared through the kitchen door without a backward glance. I wondered, idly, what she had been up to in the stables. Her duties were house duties: sweeping the floors, polishing the furniture and helping the cook. An impudent girl, my mother had called her. Left streaks of polish on the furniture and dustballs under the bed. I don't blame her, I'd replied. I'd hate to spend my days cooking and cleaning. My mother had been furious and sent me to my room.

The stable door creaked as I pushed it open, flooding the floor with a bright triangle of light.

"Ah," Joseph said, and grinned at me. "More jars." With a flick of his head he indicated a spot in the corner where I should put them.

The jars clinked as I opened the stall and stepped in. Mojo, my father's horse, snorted and rolled his eyes, and Joseph placed his hand flat on the horse's neck to hold him. Joseph's shirt, damp with perspiration, clung to his skin and his brown arms glistened in the dusty light that slid in through the narrow windows. There was an acrid, not unpleasant smell of flesh and sweat. I propped myself against the wall while Joseph reached for a brush and moved it firmly, gently, over the horse's flanks. A faint thin cry of Stephen's violin floated in on the late afternoon air. I imagined Stephen in his room, his window flung open to alert him of our father's return from the city; as soon as the car passed through the gates, the music would stop in mid-note. Stephen's long, pale fingers would slip the violin back into the case that closed with a click. He would reach for his riding clothes, his face contorted as he pulled on his leather boots and picked up the crop. Our father often complained that I, since I was tall and sturdy, should have been the boy and Stephen, who was short and always pale no matter how much time he spent in the sun, should have been the girl. Stephen's limbs were so thin I thought they would snap as easily as twigs.

"It's today, isn't it?" I asked Joseph. "Stephen has to try out Mojo?" Mojo was the strongest, most spirited horse in the stables, father had announced proudly, when he'd told Stephen he had to ride.

"First time," Joseph said. And he added softly, "Not good," and shook his head.

When Joseph and I were small, we'd been allowed to play together. Stephen used to hang around the edges of our games, bribing us with sweets or toys and sometimes we would let him join us for a while. But he balked at catching frogs or playing in the long grass for fear of snakes so we ran off, leaving him in tears. My mother would come looking for us and we'd crawl beneath the verandah, clutching each other in mock-terror as we watched her step hesitantly through the garden, pause, and turn back.

But even then Joseph was expected to sweep the floors, peel vegetables and help the gardener. I followed him around, sulking, urging him to hurry up. When my parents were out, I shelled peas or snapped beans with him. We sat on the verandah floor, bowls and baskets between us, filling our mouths with peas and spitting them out to see who could make them land the farthest.

Now, Joseph was in charge of the stables. He was not permitted to ride the horses, only to groom and feed them, but I knew he sometimes rode Mojo, bareback, in the pink and silver light before dawn. I'd wakened early one day and padded to the window and saw a horse and rider on the horizon, silhouetted against the pallid sky. Racing across the fields in the ghostly light of dawn, horse and rider could have been mythical beings, creatures from a film or a book. I wanted to fling the window open, call out a warning, but Stephen would have heard. His room was beside mine; his window faced the same direction. Some day, I told myself, I would tell Joseph that I knew his secret. I would tell him that he and Mojo looked magnificent.

Joseph moved from task to task silently, absorbed in his work. I propped myself against the wall and watched his broad hands travelling firmly, gently, over the horse's flanks. He stopped and turned to look at me and his eyes, as wide and restless as Mojo's, startled me for a moment. I wanted to put out my hand and touch him the way he touched the horse, to calm him, but the image of my pale hand against his dark skin confused me. For the first time I could remember, I shrank away from him, inside.

Joseph flung the saddle up onto Mojo's back just as we heard the sound of my father's car. The stable door swung open suddenly and my father walked in. Stephen, white around the lips, hung about behind him.

"Ready, boy?"

"Ready, *Bwana*."

We followed Joseph as he led Mojo to the paddock and held him still. Stephen placed a foot in the stirrup, slipped, stumbled and hit the side of his head against the horse's flank. Our father stood apart, motionless. His face was blank but I could see a small tic throbbing on his left cheek, just beneath his eye.

When Stephen finally settled himself in the saddle, Mojo circled the corner of the paddock slowly. He shook his head, snorted again and again. Joseph ran up, tugged at the reins and whispered something into the horse's ear. Mojo began to trot then, but Stephen didn't get far. Across the paddock and halfway back, Mojo whinnied and bucked and Stephen keeled over and tumbled to the ground. It wasn't even a spectacular fall, no cuts or broken bones that Stephen could boast about and exaggerate later. It was just a slow and foolish defeat.

Our father marched across the paddock and swung himself onto the horse while Joseph scurried to open the gate. Stephen rose slowly, his clothes dusty, his face ashen. Joseph extended his hand to help him, but Stephen grabbed his crop from the ground and raised it high.

"Stop it!" I screamed. I ran forward and wrestled the crop from his hand.

"I'll get you for this," Stephen hissed as Joseph walked away. I saw him spit on the ground as he reached the gate and then I saw shadows drifting over the fields and, overhead, clouds unfolding like dark wings.

—

"Did it rain a lot?" I asked. I'd wakened early to hear the rain rattling on the roof like pellets. Now it had stopped and the sour-sweet scent of damp earth drifted into the house. Raindrops dangled like crystals from trees and bushes in the thin morning light.

"Elizabeth." My mother raised her head from her embroidery. "You do remember you're not to go into that filthy water, don't you?"

My father, on the other side of the room, turned the page of the morning paper with a rustle that broke the stillness. A houseboy padded in with the coffee tray, arranged cups and saucers on the small table while I pondered the thread weaving in and out of the cloth my mother was holding. Pink roses the size of thumbnails, on white linen. More pillowcases. The cabinets in the room were crammed with china, porcelain figurines, glasses and crystal vases. The piano, which Stephen played only when Father was out, was littered with photographs of our family in ornate wooden frames, but the central photograph was a smiling Princess Elizabeth—who had recently been crowned queen—descending from the plane during her visit to Nairobi the year before.

I stared at my mother's head, lowered again, concentrating on a petal, at her pale fingers as they slipped the needle into the fabric, pulled it gently, patted and held it up to the window for inspection. A sudden breeze from the open door tugged at her skirt, pressed it against her ankles, slim and frail as a child's wrists.

It made me itch just to look at her stockings and high-heeled shoes. My own bare legs were tanned and marked with fine white lines and blotches from old scrapes. My wide feet were encased in my favourite worn brown sandals. I moved behind an armchair to hide them. It occurred to me then that I was a disappointment to my mother and, for a moment, the thought saddened me.

"Oh." My mother's hands fluttered and the cloth slid to the floor. My father dropped his paper and jumped to his feet. They turned. Wambui was crossing the verandah slowly, a basket of fruit on her head. Father patted Mother's shoulder. She picked up her embroidery; he reached for his paper, folded it in four and slipped it into his briefcase.

I wanted to ask them what was wrong but I knew better. Little pitchers have big ears, they would have said.

Surely they were not afraid of Wambui, a girl my own age?

—

"You all right in there?" The policeman poked his head through the window of the car. The road ahead was blocked and our boy, who for years had driven us to school without incident, was ordered out of the car. He raised his arms while another policeman slid his hands over his shirt and the pockets of his pants.

"What are they doing?" I turned to Stephen.

"Looking for Mau Mau, I expect," he muttered. He jerked his head in the boy's direction and placed a finger on his lips.

My teacher entered the classroom with a gunbelt slung around her waist. No need to be alarmed, she said. All of us have been issued revolvers, purely as a precautionary measure. She raised her hand and insisted we get on with our work. The revolver banged against her hips as she moved from desk to desk. I couldn't keep my eyes from it.

I asked Klara about it at recess.

"Mau Mau," she said and took a big bite out of her marmite sandwich.

"What Mau Mau?"

"Don't you ever read the paper or listen to the radio or anything? It's a kind of rebellion."

"What do you mean? Why?"

Klara shrugged. "They're probably fed up." She took another bite and stared at the untouched roast beef sandwich in my hand. "You going to eat that?"

I shook my head and handed her the sandwich. "Fed up with what?" I asked but Klara didn't answer. I persisted. "What do they do?"

"Chop off fingers, cut out tongues, poke out eyes. Whatever they feel like."

Then I remembered how, lately, my father had been putting away the newspapers as soon as I walked into the room, how he switched the radio off as if he didn't want me to hear the news. I imagined people who'd been tortured, holes where their eyes should have been, bloodied faces, bloodied hands. But they must have been different in the first place for something like that to have happened to them, not quite ordinary as we were.

"So what do they look like, these Mau Mau?"

"Don't be silly. They look like all the others, like your own houseboys. You can never tell."

—

"Stay on the path when you ride," our father warned. "There's been a great deal of flooding and the fields are thick with mud."

Sometimes the sun broke through a gap in the low, flat sky and lit up land that was turning into a patchwork of greens. The rains were almost over but my jars were only half-filled with frogs. I'd lost interest and had some vague idea about setting free the ones I'd captured. The rainy season seemed different this year, oppressive; it made me tired. I dragged myself around, shook my head when Joseph called, asking if I wanted to ride. I couldn't look at him or talk to him the way I'd done before, easily, as friends do. I watched him secretly, although I wasn't sure what I was looking for. Everything else seemed the same as always: foliage thickened on the dripping trees; faint, childish cries drifted in from the flooded field; Joseph emerged from the stables occasionally, leading the horses carefully along the path, to exercise them. I saw that there was a part of Joseph I knew nothing about, and this gnawed its way to the surface of my mind. With it, came an odd resentment.

One afternoon when I was lolling on my bed, my mother came into my room and placed cool fingers on my forehead.

"What's Mau Mau?" I asked, pushing her hand away.

My mother stiffened. "Troublemakers," she said. "Nothing that can't be dealt with." She passed through the door, calling over her shoulder. "Do run outside now. You've been looking quite pale."

I visited the stables later, remembering my half-formed decision to set the frogs free. I sat on the floor in the loft for a few minutes, waiting for my eyes to become accustomed to the dim light. I began to pluck the dead frogs from the jars, dropping them into a small pile at my feet. Slimy, rotting leaves clung to my fingers as I worked, and I had to keep wiping my hands on a bundle of hay. When I finished, I lay on my stomach and peered into the jars. The remaining frogs, tiny and a pale green that was almost luminous against the dense leaves, stared back at me, their marble eyes hard in their squat, ugly faces. How could I ever have thought them beautiful?

Muted giggles and the sound of rustling hay rose up from the floor below. I listened, holding my breath, then inched my way to the opening and stared down. Shadows crossed the nearest wall. Wambui rose slowly from the floor, gathering her skirt around her. Joseph lay back in the hay, grinning as he tugged playfully at her hem.

I crawled away and curled up in a corner, where the light didn't reach, until I heard them leave.

—

At night I began to listen for unusual sounds; I imagined that I saw things growing in the darkness, watching. When I finally slept, the wind passing through distant trees, or rain sliding lightly on the windows woke me as easily as if someone had gripped my shoulders and shaken me. Once, I cried out and my mother came running and folded me in her arms. A dream, I thought, in the morning, and then I saw a cup of cold milk beside my bed, covered with a frail, puckered skin. It was still early, barely light, and I lay on my bed with my face turned towards the window, staring at the steely sky. Something rattled faintly, downstairs, and I rose quietly, opened my door an inch or so and came face to face with Stephen creeping across the hall. His clothes were streaked with dirt and he was holding his mud-caked riding boots away from him. Two long scratches extended from the corner of his right eye to his ear.

"Stephen!"

"Be quiet!"

"What have you done?"

"Shut up! Shut up!" His chin quivered; tears welled up in his eyes and overflowed as he slipped into the bathroom, closing the door behind him.

"Where is he?"

Breakfast was served on the verandah on Saturday mornings. Our father's long shadow fell across the table. He inspected his rifle, tucked it under his arm and slipped the revolver that he wore each day now, into the holster on his hip.

Stephen picked up a spoon and put it down again, leaving the handle beaded with round drops of sweat. Our mother's cup clinked as she replaced it in the saucer. Her eyes skimmed over the scratches on Stephen's face, livid against his skin. I stared at the lace tablecloth, at the thin white plate in front of me, edged with gold and indigo, at the knife lying across it, its tip smeared with butter, glittering in the morning sun.

Father passed the gun to Stephen and their boots clattered as they marched across the wooden floor. The servants had gathered silently on the path, stone faces turned towards them.

"No!" I heard my voice cry out.

"Elizabeth?" My father was impatient and already halfway down the stairs.

Wambui walked away and stood apart from the others, beside the mango tree. She was quite still, impassive, her arms hanging loosely by her side. Only her eyes betrayed her. I met her dark gaze briefly, then quickly looked away.

"Nothing," I said. "It's nothing."

My father flicked his hand and the servants shuffled away.

Later, I found Mojo in the field beside the wood, lying on his side, one leg twisted under him and a faint red thread running from a small hole in the side of his head where the bullet had entered. For a moment I imagined that he was asleep and that he'd clamber up and snort, shaking off the flies that were crawling over him, their wings quivering. Shadows of hungry birds passed over me as I knelt in the mud and traced the dried blood with my finger. Nothing, I realized, would ever be the same again. Once something is known, it cannot be unknown. Forgotten perhaps, but never unknown.

When I returned from school each day I sat quietly in the house, now, reading or staring at nothing. Sometimes I pulled an atlas from my school bag and moved the tips of my fingers across Africa, then over the blue part and up to that odd, large outline: *Canada*. I whispered the words over and over again. *Canada, Canada, Africa*. They blurred, became confusing when said quickly. Canada didn't seem far away: one swift movement across the map and I was there and, just as quickly, back again. Then something cold began to spread itself inside me and I had to shut the atlas quickly and put it away. Once, I dared to ask Stephen what happened to Joseph. He looked at me slyly with his colourless eyes. There are some things, he told me, that girls shouldn't know. He had his own gun, now, and went hunting with Father at weekends.

I hadn't forgotten the frogs I'd left in the loft. They were dead, probably, their smooth skins brittle and cracked, their eyes dull. But perhaps it wasn't too late; a few sturdy ones might have survived. I could take the jars and empty them into the stream that ran along the edge of our property, and watch them swim quickly away. I imagined myself entering the musty loft, smelling the putrid smell of decaying bodies. It made me sick to think of it. Instead, I closed my heart. I was going away and I would never have to think about them again.

EVENING IN PARIS

Anna's mother is tired of another dress—her blue flowered one, this time—and has taken the scissors to it, snipped off the sleeves and the collar, unpicked the stitches on the hem. She lowers her head over the sewing machine and her black hair falls forward like wings.

The bedroom floor is a field of pale blue flowers with a small black dot in each centre. Anna leans from her bed, picks up the biggest scraps and holds them against her doll. Her doll's eyes are blue, blue as the flowers on the fabric Anna holds against her.

Anna has had to lie in bed, or at least on the bed, her mother insisted, since she was released from Nairobi General Hospital last week.

"Malaria is a serious disease," her mother says whenever Anna hears the voices of the other children and rises to peer through the window. "It is known to kill." She leans over Anna, holds a cool hand against Anna's burning forehead. "You've plenty to amuse you." With a flick of her head she indicates the picture books stacked on the side of the bed, the two scrap books of bubble gum cards—one that belongs to Anna and one that Anna's friend Teresa has let her borrow. *For one day only, mind.*

The orange cat which Anna calls Smutna—sad—is curled up at her feet. The day Anna returned from hospital the cat was hanging about in the yard, her small, sharp mouth open, emitting piteous cries.

"Mama," Anna said, "The cat is sad. I want to bring her in."

"For heaven's sake," her mother snapped. "It's just a dirty old stray. All right. All right. But don't you dare feed it. Ever."

"Mama." Anna flaps the scraps of fabric she has plucked from the floor. "Mama. Can you make a dress for my doll? Or a skirt? Can you?"

"Later, Anna. Later."

Anna folds the fabric and slips it under the bed. Her mother pushes her chair back from the sewing machine and rises to face the small, square mirror on the wall above the dresser. She smears her lips with lipstick. Her lips turn scarlet, fiery against her pale skin. She lifts the blue bottle of *Evening in Paris*, removes the gold top, dabs the perfume on the insides of her wrists, behind her ears, in the shadowy space between her breasts. She stands motionless for a moment and stares into the glass. A low sun presses in through the window and skims over her legs, her back, lightens her hair.

Threads of dust dance through the sunlight. There is a stillness in the room, something like the stillness before the rains, when the sky darkens and the air grows thick.

Anna lifts her foot and thwacks the mosquito net that hangs in a knot from the ceiling. The net swings back and forth in a most satisfactory, rhythmic way. She thwacks it again.

"Stop it, Anna," her mother cries. "You'll make it fall." She leans towards the mirror, smooths her hair, winds a dark tendril around her finger.

Anna kicks the knot again.

"Stop it," her mother repeats.

She keeps her eyes fixed on the mirror while she speaks and Anna wonders if she could be in there, a figure diminished somehow, trapped like the film stars in her scrap book who stare out with frozen faces when she flips the pages.

Her mother inspects the mole on her left cheek, touches it lightly with her forefinger. She props an elbow on the dresser and twirls her soft pencil over the mole until it is black, black as the heart of a blue flower on her dress.

She turns. "My beauty spot," she says, still holding the pencil in her hand, smiling.

—

"So that's it." Anna's mother's voice came from behind the bedroom door. It was the week before Anna was rushed to hospital. "You've decided." She had flung the small blue box Anna's father held out to her across the verandah, stepped into the bedroom and slammed the door. He followed. "That's it?" she cried. "And how much longer are we going to be stuck in this filthy place?"

Anna was sitting on the steps, drawing on the back of an envelope with wax crayons her teacher had said she could take home because they were broken. She drew a house with large flowers in a line across the front. The house was brown, the flowers orange and purple. She bent her head lower over the picture, scribbled fierce leaves on each stem. The leaves were dark blue since she had no green.

Her mother had been talking over and over about moving to Port Elizabeth. We will get a decent house, she said, with a swimming pool. A houseboy to do the cooking and cleaning. One family from this very DP camp moved there just over a year ago and already they have a house with a huge garden and two houseboys. She knows this for certain because she has written to them. They wrote back and included photographs. One photograph of a low, white house with bushes beneath the windows and beside the front doors. Another, taken from the back. More bushes and an oval pool in the centre, like a flattened egg.

"Let's wait a little." Her father's voice was so low Anna could hardly hear. "Let's wait until things are settled. We will go back. Warsaw will be different, I know, but I am sure the house is still there."

There was the creak of the closet door. Her father was reaching again for the tin box that held the ownership papers to his parents' house. He snatched them, he has said, when the bombing began and they ran from their home. He kept them in his shoes through the trek across Russia, across Persia, to the coast that brought him to Africa.

The closet door slammed shut. Now he would be flinging the lid open, grabbing the yellowed papers, waving them in the air.

Anna scrambled up, picked up the blue box her mother had thrown on the floor. Slowly, she pushed the bedroom door open.

"Mama." She held out the box. "Open this. It may be something nice."

"All right, Anna," her mother replied, her voice soft. She reached for the box, opened it, took out the small blue bottle with the golden top.

"*Evening in Paris*," she said. She laughed. She dropped the bottle on the dresser, beside a photograph of herself and Anna's father. The photograph was taken the day they were married, not long after they met in the camp, the year the war ended.

—

"That cat is too fat for a stray." Anna's mother flicks on the bedroom light, draws the curtains on a blackening sky.

Anna picks up Smutna, carries her out onto the verandah where her father is sitting with a bottle on the table and a glass in his hand. The cat's fur is softer, thicker than when she first found her, her stomach round. Anna leaves scraps for her under the verandah steps every day—bits of egg, bread, a piece of sausage, a slice of mango or papaya sometimes. Milk in a small cracked bowl she hopes her mother hasn't noticed is missing.

"You're sure you won't come with us?" Anna's mother calls.

Her father raises his glass to his lips.

Teresa's Uncle Tadeusz, who lives right in Nairobi, not in the camp, is taking Teresa's parents to a film in his new car. The car is big and black, and shone in the low light as he drove earlier through the dust road, towards the camp.

"Come with us," he waved to Anna's parents as he walked by.

Her father shook his head. Her mother waved back. "All right," she called.

Now her heels click across the verandah, there's a swish of her skirt, and she disappears into the darkness. There are voices, laughter, the sound of a car starting, pulling away. Anna lowers herself on the steps and arranges Smutna on her lap. She glances at her father, hidden in the shadows.

Sometimes he rises at nine o'clock and heads for the living room, to listen to the news on the BBC. Since last year, when Anna started school and began to learn English, he has asked her to listen with him.

"Stay with me," he begs as he fiddles with the knob on the wireless. "Listen. Tell me if I miss something important." There's a crackle, a screech. He continues fiddling until he hears the deep voice of the announcer. Anna settles cross-legged on the hard floor. She sighs, raises her eyes to the ceiling.

Important, she knows, is any mention of Poland, any information about what is happening there. She knows that Stalin is an old man and won't last forever. She knows that when he dies they will all go to Warszawa, to live in the grey brick house that belongs to her father's family. The house has a huge garden with apple trees and rose bushes and so many rooms you can get lost in it, not like the chicken coop they live in now.

Her father is certain that the house is still there, as certain as he is that though his parents are dead, his younger sister is still alive and looking for him, just as he is looking for her. He writes often to the Red Cross and, although the letters they send back make him cover his face with his hands, he knows they'll find her eventually. She was seven years old the last time he saw her, in 1939. She is twenty-one now, a young woman. Her name, too, is Anna.

He stares over the railings when he talks about his home. He inspects the moon, a piece of bone in the sky. He pulls Anna towards him, twists her lank, pale hair between his fingers.

"Anna?" He shakes his head. Anna holds her breath. "You don't look like her," he says.

Teresa bounces up and down on the end of Anna's bed.

"I have more cards than you," Anna says. "Swap?"

The one card she would like from Teresa is the Clark Gable, the only one she doesn't have. Clark Gable is smiling in the card, laughing almost, and seems about to wink. If Teresa agrees to a swap, Anna will have to offer something special. The Robert Mitchum, perhaps—the man Teresa claims makes her clamp her hand on her chest and keel over.

"He's ugly," Anna says but Teresa tells her she doesn't know anything.

Well, he is ugly, Anna thinks. She has two cards of him, exactly the same, one in her scrap book, the other in the tattered chocolate box beneath her bed. Robert Mitchum is wearing a wide-brimmed hat that throws a shadow over his eyes. His collar is turned up around his neck as if he is trying to hide.

She has other cards in the box that are also duplicates of the ones in the scrap book: Lauren Bacall, Roy Rogers, Ava Gardner, Dirk Bogart, Rita Hayworth. She takes them out sometimes when she's alone, pairs the men with the women and lays them out two by two. But she keeps Robert Mitchum away from Ava Gardner. Ava Gardner has stiff pink lace wrapped around bare shoulders and a cool marble face. Although she isn't smiling, she is the most beautiful woman Anna owns. She reminds her of her mother.

"Swap you Robert Mitchum for Clark Gable," Anna says. "And next time we play castles you have to let Marek be my prince."

"Go with Feliks," Teresa snorts, whenever they play. She grabs Marek's arm for herself. Marek makes up the games they all play. He snaps his fingers and tosses his dark hair when he explains the rules. Feliks has a pale, round face and sucks his thumb when he thinks no one is looking. His hair is the same colour as the red dusty earth in the camp. Sometimes his mother sends him out with a bobby pin holding back his curls, and everyone points and snickers.

"You won't give me your Robert Mitchum, I know. You're just teasing." Teresa picks up her scrap book and holds it against her chest. "You're stupid."

"I could. I have two. Look, I'll show you." Anna jumps down from the bed, kneels on the floor to reach the chocolate box.

Her father buys bubble gum whenever he is in Nairobi. He extracts the flat, sweet-smelling packets from his pocket when he returns, holds each one up between two fingers. He smiles, pretends he doesn't know how they got there.

Whenever Tadeusz visits, Teresa grabs his arm. "Did you bring bubble gum?" she asks.

Sometimes he does, but usually he brings fabric and hair ribbons for Teresa and her older sister, Kasia. He also brings chocolates in long black and gold boxes, handfuls of flowers, baskets of fruit, packets of cigarettes. He has given Kasia a thin silver necklace and Teresa a silver charm bracelet with a rickshaw dangling from it, a tiger, a parasol and a small rose with petals as thin as a baby's fingernails. He brought Teresa's mother an ivory necklace which she wears to Mass every Sunday. The beads are small and yellowed, the size of birds' eggs.

My Uncle Tadeusz, Teresa often boasts, escaped from Poland during the war with lots of money and gold. He plans to live in England. He has applied already but when he had his medical he was refused because his right leg is half an inch shorter than his left and he walks with a limp unless he wears a special shoe. He is going to apply again and if he is refused, he will try Canada, Australia or America. Some country will definitely take him because he is rich.

Anna is on her knees, reaching for the chocolate box, when the bedroom door is flung open. Kasia slips in and closes the door behind her. "What are you two up to?" She smiles. She crosses the room and lies back on the double bed, raises a leg slowly, turns it this way and that, inspects it carefully, lowers it again. She yawns. Kasia is fourteen and has breasts. She placed her finger over her lips one day when Teresa and Anna were playing with their cutout dolls and pulled up her shirt.

"Look," she said. Her breasts are small, tight mounds, not like Anna's mother's which are large and soft and shift beneath her clothes when she moves. Anna saw her father come up behind her mother in the kitchen once as she raised her arms to reach for flour on the top shelf. His fingers brushed the buttons of her blouse and she turned quickly, her lips thin, her eyes bright in her flushed face.

"I have a secret," Kasia says. She arches her back.

Teresa stares at her. "I know all about it. Dad's going to be mad when he finds out. You're stupid."

"What do you know?" Kasia laughs. "You're just a little kid. Besides, he's given me a dress, one of his mother's. A proper dress, from a shop. Yellow silk with pearl buttons all the way down the back. His mother will never miss it. She's got thousands."

"Dad will kill you. You know what they say about the English boys."

"What?" Anna sits up. "What?"

"Shut up." Teresa yanks the door open. "Shut up, Anna. You don't know anything."

"What do they say about the English boys?" Anna asks her father one evening.

Her father places his glass on the verandah table and peers at her. In the fading light he seems to be receding, moving backwards underwater.

"Who've you been talking to?" he asks.

"Nobody. I just want to know."

"They're different, that's all."

"How?"

"They have things. Money. Cars." He waves a hand in the air. "And so on."

Anna sits on the steps and stares into the blackness. The bottle, her father's glass, clink through the night noises, the wind sifting through long grasses and leaves, the cackle of a hyaena in the distance. A round, transparent moon slides out from behind a cloud that has strung itself out like a veil. Moonlight touches the ground, the low, squat trees, the square houses with their windows and doors closed, muffled.

Her father once told her he's afraid only of things he cannot see. She shivers, strains to see through the shadows, through dark shapes that make no sense.

"We're all going dancing," her mother had said earlier. "Tadeusz has found a wonderful place. Come with us if you want." She turned quickly, held up her hands while the red dress she had just finished making skimmed and flared around her thighs.

"Where did you get the fabric?" Anna's father asked.

"Tadeusz," she replied. She dabbed *Evening in Paris* in the space between her breasts. Small, dark stains appeared on the dress.

"You shouldn't have taken it. That man is dirt."

"At least he's alive," she replied. She brushed past him, past Anna, and slipped through the door.

—

Marek has devised a new game from a film he has seen about warriors who must eat the flesh of their victims in order to become full members of their tribe.

"Hold this," he says and hands Teresa a thick slice of bread. "Men," he shouts, "if you want to be members of the tribe, do this." He holds up his penknife, slits the tip of his thumb open. He tears a small piece of bread, presses it against the wound to soak up the blood. He swallows the bread and passes the knife to the boy beside him. One by one each boy does the same. Feliks throws up over his sandals as soon as the blood begins to spurt from his thumb and runs home while the others jeer.

"He's gone and spoiled everything," Teresa cries. "Now we can't play."

"I'll do it," Anna says. "I'll do it instead. I'm not scared."

She will cut herself, swallow her own blood. The knife is sharp, quick. It won't hurt at all. Whenever she falls and grazes her knees, the beads of blood that squeeze through the slashed skin shine dark and thick like jewels.

"Marek." She holds out her hand for the knife.

"I want to play something else," Teresa shouts. She stamps her foot. "Right now. Right now."

Anna walks away and sits on her steps. Her mother emerges from the kitchen with a towel draped over one shoulder and a large white bowl in her hands. She sinks to the ground, peers beneath the steps, reaches in, scoops up a kitten, then another and another. She drops them into the bowl. Two are white, one black, two more are orange, like Smutna. Their eyes are closed and they writhe, push against one another. Anna leans over to stroke them but her mother takes the towel and stretches it over the bowl. There is a cry from beneath the house. Anna bends over to look but can see nothing.

"What are you doing?" she asks.

"We're going to be overrun with cats," her mother replies as she walks away with the bowl, towards the river. "She'll be better off without them."

—

When they leave the church after Mass on Sunday, Tadeusz strolls towards them. He leans over Anna. "Hey," he says. "Want to go see *Snow White and the Seven Dwarfs*? There's a matinee this afternoon." He looks over Anna's head at her parents. "We could all go out for something to eat afterwards, then I'll drive you home."

Anna squints into the sun. The skirt of her mother's blue-flowered dress dances in the breeze. Her father is a rigid silhouette against the white church that is baking in the sunlight. "You three go." He nods curtly, then he's gone, head down, hands in his pockets, towards the bus stop.

Tadeusz buys Anna a strawberry ice cream cornet in the theatre. She holds it in her hand so long, it melts and drips over her knees and makes them sticky. She begins to cry as soon as Snow White leans over the wishing well and sees her reflection in the water, and she can't stop. When the film ends and the lights go on she turns away so her mother and Tadeusz can't see her red eyes, but they notice anyway. They laugh.

"Don't be silly," her mother says. "The film ended happily, didn't it?"

Tadeusz takes them to a restaurant where he and Anna's mother drink tea from cups with tiny yellow flowers around the rim. They whisper, smile at each other. The tips of their fingers touch as they pass the sugar bowl, the milk jug.

There is Coca-Cola for Anna, in a bottle of thick glass, tinted green, and a straw that bobs up and down when she tries to drink. Bubbles rush to her nose and make her eyes water as she sips. Her stomach flips. She slides from the chair and runs through the swinging doors, through the next door that has a picture of a stick woman painted on the front, and throws up in the toilet. She lowers the lid and sits down. She thinks of her mother rising from the table, looking around, hurrying through the swinging doors, calling, *Anna. Anna. Are you all right?* She will lean over, place a cool hand on Anna's forehead, smile.

She stares at the white walls while she waits, at the white ceiling, at the door with the sharp nail sticking out from the broken lock.

When she has sat so long her legs are numb, she jumps up and slams the palm of her hand against the nail. She stares at the puncture on the skin, a pink dot, at the stunned patch of white around it. The dot suddenly gushes red. She returns to the restaurant with toilet paper wrapped around her hand, red bleeding through.

"For heaven's sake, Anna. How did you do that?"

"A nail." She looks down at her feet while Tadeusz takes her hand, removes the paper, wraps her hand in a starched white handkerchief he produces from his pocket, secures it with a knot. She stares out of the car window on the way home, at the sun, a wild, swirling orange hurtling towards the horizon. She sees the reflection of her thin pale hair, tangled in the breeze. She thinks of Snow White, of her dark, smooth hair, her white skin and deep red lips, and of how the prince fell in love with her the moment he saw her.

—

"Tonight we're going to a film," Anna's mother calls from the bedroom. "Why don't you come?"

She's going alone with Tadeusz this time because Teresa's parents are too busy packing, now, to bother with nights out. They have been relocated. They are moving to England. We'll see spring in England, they keep saying. They smile. England is beautiful in spring. They know because they have seen pictures: daffodils, tulips, soft green grass on gentle hills—nothing like this parched earth they've had to suffer all these years.

"You go," Anna's father calls back. "I'll keep an eye on Anna. Have a good time."

The evenings that her mother goes out, Anna's father sits in the shadows of the verandah with his bottle and his glass. She perches on the steps while he talks of snow, of ice so cold it turns to fire when touched with a bare finger. Moonlit frost on railings, on roofs, on the branches of leafless trees.

He talks of his little sister, Anna, who had a black and white rabbit she called Jan Sobieski, after a famous king. She played the piano and everyone said she showed great promise. She played often for gatherings with family and friends. She perched on the stool, bit her lip and frowned at the music score. Her dark hair settled on her shoulders in fat curls.

One night they all rushed out into the street when the bombs began to fall. Halfway down the block, a wall of brick collapsed on their parents. He managed to grab Anna and pull her back, but lost her later in the panicked crowd.

He doesn't speak at all tonight. The air is dense and damp and a hot wind billows onto the verandah.

"What time is it?" Anna asks.

"I don't know." He peers at his watch. "Nine. Just after. Go to bed, Anna."

"Let's listen to the news first. Come on, Tatus. Come on."

He turns his head away. She slips into the living room, twists the knob on the wireless until the crackling and wheezing fade and she hears that deep voice. She sits on the floor and wraps her arms about her knees. She stares above the radio, at the shadows on the wall, and thinks she can see the war, a vague, amorphous shape, a cloud that has done its damage and has drifted away and dissolved.

Her eyes are beginning to close when the voice announces that Stalin is dead.

Joseph Stalin, the most powerful leader in the history of Russia, died from a stroke tonight in Moscow. An elite team of doctors worked around the clock, trying to save his life. Stalin was 73. Joseph Stalin, the voice repeats, *dead from a stroke at the age of 73.*

Anna doesn't know what a stroke is but imagines it as a blow, or lightning that zigzags through the sky towards its target. Joseph. Josef. It never occurred to her that he had a first name, like an ordinary person. Was this Joseph tall or short? Fair or dark? She tries to remember if her father ever showed her pictures of him in a newspaper. Did he have a wife? A little girl? She closes her eyes and presses them hard against her knees. Oranges and reds explode, shatter.

When she opens the door to the verandah there is a sour-sweet smell of damp earth. The rain has begun with a slow, soft flow.

She shakes her father's arm. "Stalin is dead. Stalin is dead." She tugs his hand. His fingers are cold. Raindrops fall harder, rattle on the roof like pellets.

"Tatus, it's all right now. Stalin is dead."

He raises a hand, drops it on his lap. "I'm tired," he whispers.

His head is flung back, his eyes closed. Anna drags a blanket from the bedroom and covers him from his neck down to his feet. A soaked Smutna appears and rubs herself against Anna's leg. Anna picks her up and carries her into the bedroom, tries to place her on the bed beside her doll. But Smutna digs her claws into Anna's arm and makes small, soft noises as if she's forgotten about her kittens, about the way she cried in the darkness beneath the house.

In the dull light, the cat's fur seems exactly the same colour as Feliks' hair. Feliks picked her up earlier, when Anna was sitting outside with Smutna on her lap. He reached for the cat and lifted her onto his shoulder.

"From far away," Anna had said, "I don't know if I could tell the difference between the two of you."

They'd both laughed.

Teresa emerged from her house, carrying her scrap book. "What's so funny?" she asked.

"Nothing," Anna replied.

"Here." Teresa thrust her scrap book at Anna. "I don't want this. We're going to England, you know, and I'm supposed to take only what is really important. We'll buy plenty of stuff when we get there, my dad says. And here." She handed over a bundle of yellow fabric. "Kasia says you might as well have the dress."

—

Anna wraps Smutna in the yellow silk dress and places her on the bed. She puts Teresa's scrap book aside without checking for Clark Gable. She sits on the floor, reaches under the bed for the chocolate box and the pieces of fabric splattered with blue flowers. She crumples the fabric and pushes it aside. She removes Ava Gardner from the chocolate box, picks up Robert Mitchum and places her beside him.

They look fine together. She can't figure out why she never thought of this before.

RUNNING AWAY

Emilia was seven the first time she ran away, the time the Masai man brought her back. It was the day after she, her parents and her twin brothers had been to St. George's School in Nairobi, for the annual celebration of the feast of St. George, the patron saint of England. She wore her Sunday dress—pale blue satin with lace around the hem, white socks and white, shiny shoes. The twins, Jan and Jakub, who, at eleven, were in the senior class, were also in their Sunday clothes—navy shorts, white shirts and ties.

"Get lost," they hissed in her ear as the bus pulled up beside the school and they climbed out. "Get lost. We hate girls."

Emilia sat down at one of the long wooden tables that had been set out in the quadrangle.

A lady appeared, holding a plate. "You're one of our displaced persons, aren't you?" she said. She smiled, leaned forward and touched Emilia's pale hair. "My, but aren't you pretty," she added. She deposited a fork and a slice of white cake with yellow icing in front of Emilia. There were small silver balls, smaller than marbles, scattered through the icing.

Her parents were walking about. They inspected the decorations on the walls and windows. Her father, hands clasped behind his back, in the dark suit that was shiny at the elbows, was as stiff as one of the twins' wooden soldiers. Her mother looked very fine in the purple dress she had made for the occasion. She smiled and nodded at the English parents, at the teachers.

There were paper cutouts of golden crowns, studded with jewels, on each classroom window. There were paper flowers stuck to the glass.

Balloons on strings were attached to doorknobs, to pillars. They bounced about in the breeze. In the centre of the quadrangle, on a large board, was a poster of St. George facing a green dragon. The dragon's mouth was open to reveal white, sharp teeth. St. George was short, his shoulders narrow. His sword was wide, pointed, as large as St. George himself. The dragon loomed over him, spewing fire.

"Smile," someone sang out. Emilia looked up at a man who had a brown box pressed to his face. She tried to smile through a mouthful of cake. The man lowered the camera and fiddled with a knob.

She plucked out the silver balls and placed them in a row on the side of her plate, for later. One she had missed was stuck between her teeth and she was prodding it with a finger when she heard the camera click.

"For heaven's sake." Her mother's hand was on her arm. "That's rude."

When they were back at the DP camp, the twins shouted through the window. "Come on, Emilia. Come play."

"Come on," their friends echoed. "Play with us."

"Go on, then," Emilia's mother said. "Go. No point in changing out of your good clothes now. It will be dark in an hour or so, and bedtime. Be careful. Don't get dirty."

The low sun sent yellow rays across the camp. Emilia cast a long, thin shadow. A transparent moon was suspended in a sky as blue as her dress. The boys were lined up darkly beside the ditch ahead.

She walked towards them. One grabbed her hand.

"March," he yelled. "March, men, march. We have our hostage."

We're playing war, Emilia thought. The boys always played war. They had sticks for guns. "Bang bang," they shouted. They hurled stones and threw themselves on the ground. "Boom," they shrieked.

She wondered why they had never asked her to play before as they led her towards the bushes near the Masai camp. The bushes seemed darker and bigger than ever. She tried to pull back but the grip on her wrist tightened.

"Off," the boys chanted as they dragged her behind a thick bush. "Off, off."

One pushed her onto the ground, lifted her skirt and pulled down her knickers. He spread her legs. Twigs and stones pricked her bum.

"Jan. Jakub," she cried. Her brothers' faces rose above her, white and distant as moons.

"Go on, Edmund. Do it," the boys yelled. "We dare you."

Edmund stepped back. He was shorter than the others. His carrot-coloured hair spilled over his eyes. His belly was round, his arms and legs white sticks.

"OK, don't. But you can't be in the gang any more. You're a coward, that's what."

Edmund began to unfasten his belt. Emilia saw his hands tremble. She closed her eyes. He landed on top of her and she felt something hard and damp between her legs. Rubbing, rubbing. His breath was hot on her face.

When he scrambled up, there was a cheer. Emilia opened her eyes. Edmund was fastening his pants, grinning into his shoulder.

"Don't you dare tell or we'll get you." Jakub stood over her. "Here, put your knickers on and go home." He flung them on her face. Someone snickered.

When she sat up the boys were gone. Footsteps thudded faintly in the distance and then there was silence. She dressed herself, rubbed dirt from her clothes as best as she could, wiped the sticky stuff from between her legs with leaves.

The sky had blackened. Trees and shrubs loomed like shadows. She saw the flicker of fire at the Masai camp. She stood behind a tree and watched. Dark silhouettes squatted around flames that twisted orange and red. Voices rose in song, low and comforting, a hum. She was sure she could feel the warmth of the flames from where she stood. If she entered the camp, sat down beside one of the dark figures, joined in the singing, would anyone notice, she wondered.

"Oh, Emilia," her mother cried as Emilia climbed the verandah steps, "I've been worried sick. The boys returned ages ago. They said they didn't know where you were. And look what you've done to your dress."

Emilia's father was at the table, cutting a long thin shape from a newspaper. Snip, snip. He held the cutting up to the light, lowered it over a blank page in his scrap book. Emilia could see an upside down picture at the top of the strip of paper above the lines and lines of writing. The man in the picture was dressed the way her father was dressed in the photograph on the living room wall. Her father had been in the army then. A cap was pulled over his eyes, a stiff collar around his neck. Medals dangled from one side of his chest.

He looked up over his glasses as her mother grabbed Emilia's shoulders and turned her around. "Listen to your mother," he said.

The twins emerged from their bedroom and faced her, arms folded across their chests.

"Emilia, just look at the back of this dress," their mother continued. "Your Sunday dress and I don't know if I'll ever get the stains out. And you've torn the lace. Right here. You're a wicked girl."

She felt the sting of her mother's palm on the back of her bare legs just as Jan mouthed, "You dare."

58

Next day, Emilia hacked two slices of bread from the loaves her mother had left to cool on the kitchen table. She spread them with jam and pressed them into a sandwich. She took the long sausage from the cupboard, sliced a piece and held it up for inspection before wrapping it in her handkerchief. She was pleased with the neatness of the cut. It was as good as her mother's. She filled an empty milk bottle with water and packed it all in Jakub's old battered satchel.

The sun was high as she headed out, and she grabbed her straw hat. She passed the twins. They were sneaking under the house, clutching cigarettes she'd seen them pinch earlier from their father's jacket pocket.

She bent over and peered in. There were three other boys there, sitting cross-legged among the thick stilts.

"Good-bye," she called to her brothers.

"Hey, it's your stupid sister," one of the boys hissed. "Here, show us your knickers."

There was laughter, the strike of a match. "You dare tell and you're for it," Jakub snapped."

"I won't. I'm running away."

"Good. Don't come back."

Jan pointed a finger at her. "Bang bang," he said.

Years later, Emilia sees it all as a story, a dream. She sees the child from behind: trudging along the road, sandalled feet stirring up small puffs of red dust, pale hair fluttering around her shoulders, beneath the straw hat. As she walks, she shields her eyes to see the antelopes, the majestic curved horns on their heads. They are prancing in the distance on dainty dancing feet, heading towards the horizon. Antelopes, she has heard, together with other creatures, live in another land just over the horizon.

Emilia followed the road, skipping. She walked past the Gromykos' house, past the Skibas' and the Nowakowskis'. Old Pani Nowakowska—the witch—was limping towards the outhouse. She leaned on her cane with one hand, hitched up her skirt in preparation to reveal a mottled thigh with the other. She stopped and pointed her cane like a gun at Emilia. Emilia ran. When she looked back, the corrugated metal roofs of the houses in the camp blinked in the sun.

Over on the right, in the distance, the low white houses of the British filtered through trees and shrubs that seemed to flower forever; they were settled on the hillside like satisfied birds.

"Bougainvillea, hibiscus, frangipani, oleander," Emilia chanted as she skipped. She liked the song-like sounds of the foreign words. She knew them well because, along with discarded clothes, her mother sometimes brought cuttings from the gardens of the British ladies for whom she sewed.

Her mother left the cuttings in water for weeks and planted them in the hard earth of the yard as soon as they sprouted roots. "I'll show them we're as good as anybody," she said. "We're just as good." She watered the plants daily, repeated their names like a litany and watched them as if they were babies, then stamped her foot and yanked them up when they turned brown.

Emilia ate the sandwich later, on the bank of the river. She held up the sausage and wondered if she should save it. Her eyelids drooped. The sun began its descent from the sky. Her feet burned and she removed her sandals and wriggled her toes. The river was low, the banks dry. The river water made a sound like a tap left running as it trickled over stones. The long grass whispered in the breeze. She lay back, and closed her eyes.

Wish, wish, wish, the grass said.

Why does the river run? she wondered.

Where does it go?

Why does the sun spin and spin?

When she opened her eyes the sky was dark. One long strip of red remained above the horizon. A shadow was squatting beside her.

"Come," the shadow said. His eyes were large and turned up slightly at the sides, as if he were smiling. The whites were very white.

The Masai man with the smiling eyes, she called him later, to her mother's annoyance.

He stood. He was as tall as a tree. He lifted her with his long arms and hoisted her over his hip. She leaned against his chest and his beads pressed against her cheek as he walked. Even in the darkness, the colours of his beads were clear. Red, blue, yellow, orange. He felt his way with a stick through the grass, across the rocks and stones. He was warm. He smelled warm.

Every window in the camp was lit and people were scurrying back and forth. There was shouting. When they got closer, Emilia heard her name over and over.

"Emilia! Emilia!"

At the edge of the camp the Masai man lowered her to the ground and took her hand. She gripped it hard. He looked down, nodded, smiled. When they reached the first house Emilia's mother ran towards them, crying.

"The boys said you ran away. We've been frantic. You are a wicked girl."

A crowd gathered. Emilia turned and buried her face in the man's hand. Her mother yanked her away.

"Thank you," she said. Her voice was cold and tight. "Thank you very much. Go now." She flapped her hand at the Masai man. "Go on."

He stepped back and disappeared into the shadows.

Emilia was in bed later and almost asleep when she heard her parents whisper.

"When I was giving her a bath," her mother said, "she told me she was afraid."

There was a pause, then a rustle of paper and the snip, snip of her father's scissors. "What is she afraid of?" he asked.

"She wouldn't say."

"Well. There is danger out there, you know."

—

Emilia is fifteen and is planning to run for the second time. Her plans, however, are vague. After too long in a cramped flat her parents have bought a semi in a suburb of Manchester. The house is built of brick that once must have been pink but is now covered with grey film from the soot spewed from distant factory chimneys so tall they almost touch the clouds. There is a patch of garden in front of the house where a previous owner planted roses that struggle to open their faces in the bleakness. There is a large square of very green grass in the back, a coalshed and a doghouse covered with moss. These are surrounded by a tall brick wall. A thin, dark river runs beyond the backyard.

Emilia likes to stand on the riverbank. She looks down at the thick water. Toffee papers, plastic bags, cigarette cartons float by. She wonders where they go.

"Look," Emilia's mother said, the day they moved in. She flung the back door open. Her voice was hard. "We're on the waterfront." She laughed, buried her face in her handkerchief.

Their elderly neighbour leaned over the wall as they clattered about. "I heard you talking. You some more of them DPs?" he shouted. "They're all over the place. I don't have a problem with you lot but I don't want no trouble. All right?"

"Do we have to live here?" Emilia asked. "I don't like it."

"You take what you can get," her mother replied. "During the war we had to run and run. You run wherever you can. Be grateful."

The doctor prescribes pills to help Emilia sleep. Sixty-eight, sixty-nine, seventy, she counts.

"I have trouble getting to sleep," she'd told him. "If I do sleep, I wake in the middle of the night."

His pen had scratched the paper as he'd written the prescription. He'd torn the paper from the pad. "Call me when you run out," he had said, without looking at her.

The pills are small, round, white. So very small. Emilia wonders how anything so small can have an effect.

She takes one, occasionally, on the worst nights, calls the doctor for more, tells him she has run out. He prescribes twenty-five at a time.

She pours them out of the container sometimes, dividing them into piles of ten. Seventy. She smiles. A nice round number. She carries them with her wherever she goes.

When Emilia's father returns from the coal mine his face is grey with coal dust. He bathes, puts on clean clothes and, after supper, retreats to the living room with his scissors, his newspaper, a scrap book and bottle of glue.

Since they moved to England, he's been able to buy *Dziennik Polski* from the corner shop every day. He counts himself lucky. He is now on his seventh scrap book. He nods, thanks the shopkeeper regularly for keeping this particular newspaper on order.

He has covered one wall in the living room with medals, framed and behind glass. He has hung up cuttings from newspapers, yellowed with age, photographs of men in uniform, men marching in a line or standing to attention, guns slung over their shoulders.

The two most recent photographs—the only ones in colour—were taken in a studio in Manchester a year ago. One is of Jakub, one of Jan. They are in their soldiers' uniforms. Flat caps, short-sleeved shirts, chins lifted high above stiff collars.

Although there has not been conscription in England for years, the boys insisted on joining the army as soon as they finished school. They are now stationed in Germany.

Their father gazes at their photographs with pride. "Good men," he mutters. "Good men."

Emilia hopes they both step on a bomb.

—

Emilia's mother works at a delicatessen in a small shopping centre four blocks from their house where, she says, the district suddenly becomes very nice. There are tall trees on the streets and the houses are huge.

Emilia stops off sometimes after school when she is needed to help carry groceries home. Her mother smiles, laughs, jokes with the customers while Emilia sits on a hard chair in the corner and waits for the store to close.

Her mother's face is grey as porridge. Dark half-moons are stamped beneath her eyes. She rises at dawn each day and is in the store by seven, although it doesn't open until nine.

"I have to stack shelves, wash the floor and so on," she says when Emilia tells her she should sleep a little longer. "I like everything to be ready when Mr. Greenfield comes."

The store sells *pierogi, barszcz* in small plastic containers, *sernik*—cheesecake, by the slice. The British ladies pore over the small words on cans and jars. They frown. They smile and nod at Emilia's mother.

"Marta," they say. "How do I serve this? So exotic."

"What exactly is in this jar, Marta? It looks very interesting."

"You know I love to try something different."

Emilia's mother hurries over, her cheeks pink with pride.

Her favourite customer is Mrs. Roberts, a tall woman with a loud voice and blonde hair piled high on her head. Her daughter, Pamela, is in Emilia's class at school.

"Mrs. Roberts is the wife of a doctor. A psychiatrist," her mother says. "Do you know, they live only a couple of blocks away. You must have seen them at ten o'clock Mass at St. Paul's. She always says hello."

"I have seen them," Emilia replies. Dr. Roberts, of the cool marble eyes. Mrs. Roberts with pointed pink fingernails.

Her mother nods and smiles, at church. Emilia is afraid she will curtsy. Her face burns at the thought.

Sometimes Emilia's mother brings home a bag of clothes Mrs. Roberts has given her. Clothes that don't fit her any more, clothes that Pamela, her daughter, has discarded.

"Give them away," Emilia says.

Mr. Greenfield, the boss at the shop, a short man whose dark hair shines with Brylcreem, slips Emilia's mother a can of ham, a jar of sauerkraut or beets from time to time. "How did I ever get so lucky," he says, "to have found someone like you who understands all this foreign stuff?"

Emilia's mother smiles and smiles. The boss turns to Emilia, raises an eyebrow and winks. She lowers her head, smooths her pale straight hair forward over her face.

She would like to leap up, knock down the cans and jars her mother has arranged so precisely on the shelves, hurl them through the window.

"Do you have to work there?" she asks as they walk home.

"Emilia! What do you mean?"

"Well, everybody's so, you know, condescending."

"Condescending. What is condescending?"

"Well, you know. They act as if you're pathetic. *Jaka ty jestes pate-tyczna.*"

"What on earth are you blabbing about? Mr. Greenfield is grateful for the work I do. Look." She stops and drags a jar of pickles from her shopping bag.

Polskie Ogorki, the label reads. "See. He gave me this, just today. He treats me the way he would treat anybody. I sometimes wonder if you understand anything."

—

"Emilia is one of our displaced persons," the nun said as she ushered Emilia into the classroom. "I would like you all to be kind to her."

That was five years ago. Emilia had been ten and it was her second day in England. She'd spent the first day with her head stuck out of the window of their flat, trying to see beyond the swirling fog. She thought she was trapped forever in a stifling cloud.

Next morning, a lady with a stern face and brown lace-up shoes appeared at the door. Emilia's mother smiled, pushed Jan and Jakub forward, tightened the hair ribbons on Emilia's braids.

"Go on," she said.

The lady held Emilia's hand as they walked to the school. Jan and Jakub marched on ahead. At one side of the building, the twins were greeted by a man in a black robe and white collar. The lady guided Emilia to the other side. *Juniors*, was written above the door.

Emilia hung her head as the nun led her to the front of the classroom. The eyes frightened her. So many eyes! She stared at her black shoes. Her mother had polished them earlier, and they shone in the dull light. The drone of a lawn mower came through the open window. The fresh, sweet scent of newly-cut grass billowed in.

She had heard her Nairobi teacher talk about misplaced crayons, erasers, pencils. One English word so often seemed like another.

Displaced.

"Why do you talk so funny?" one of the girls asked her that day, at playtime.

Emilia shook her head. Her brothers were darting across the asphalt, behind the fence that separated *Juniors* from *Seniors*. Half a dozen other boys raced with them. All crouched, pointed sticks.

"Bang bang," she heard.

The woman with the stern face was waiting at the gate at four o'clock, home time. She took Emilia's hand. Jan and Jakub hung around behind with the boys they had met.

"Hey, that's your sister?" she heard. There was a whistle, another. "Did she really? Honestly? With anyone? Wow."

"Here, a couple of ciggies," a boy would say in the camp in Nairobi. He'd hand them to Jan and Jakub.

Sometimes a bottle would be exchanged with a small amount of clear liquid at the bottom and the twins would grab Emilia and hustle her behind the bush near the Masai camp. She no longer struggled and cried. It only took a few minutes, after all.

"Did you really? When you lived in Africa?" a girl asks. "I think it's disgusting."

The question tires her, she has heard it so often.

"Who told you?"

"I don't remember. But everybody knows. Everybody thinks you're terrible. I think it's awful. Besides, it's a mortal sin. You'll go to hell. See if you don't."

They are sitting on a bench outside the cloakroom. The girl's name is Janet or Janice or Jen. All faces, all names, all voices are the same.

Emilia looks up.

Why are the clouds in an English sky always low and thick? she wonders.

Why is the sun pale yellow, like a blob of custard?

A year ago, the day before Jan and Jakub left, the family had a celebration dinner.

Father wore his uniform. Medals dangled above his pocket. Emilia thought he smelled as if he had been rolling about in a dank cellar.

Mother cooked everything: *barszcz, pierogi, bigos, golabki*. She ran to and from the kitchen carrying trays, platters.

"I am so proud of my sons," she cried. She placed her hands on Jan's broad shoulders, then Jakub's.

They sat around the fireplace after they had eaten. They pulled out photograph albums, started with baby pictures, flipped through the pages. Jan and Jakub, one year old, heads together, grinning into the camera. A naked baby Emilia on her stomach, barely able to hold up her head.

Their father dabbed the corners of his eyes with his handkerchief.

Later photographs of the boys in their Sunday best on the white church steps in Nairobi, the day of their First Communion. Emilia, a small cutout figure, leans against the white church wall behind them. She is sucking a strand of hair.

"Oh, Emilia," her mother cried, her index finger on the photograph. "What are we to do with you?"

She turned to the photographs taken at the school on St. George's Day. Jan and Jakub are facing the camera, smiling. Their ties are straight.

Emilia is eating the white cake with yellow icing. She has a finger in her mouth; she's trying to dislodge the small silver ball stuck between her teeth, and smile at the same time.

"Emilia," her mother says. "The only photo we have of you on that special day and you ruined it."

"Yeah, Emilia." Jakub grins. "You are very, very wicked."

Every day now, it seems, Jen or Janice or Janet reaches towards Emilia with her pale, pudgy hand. Jen's black rosary beads dangle from the side of her belt, like a nun's. When she blinks, which she often does, Emilia can see specks of dandruff in her curly eyelashes.

Jen is going to enter. Everyone says so. She wants to save souls. The nuns invite her for tea on Holy Days.

"You must repent," Jen tells Emilia. "Remember the parable of the shepherd and the lost sheep? Remember Mary Magdalen?"

Emilia turns away, bows her head. She hopes she looks repentant so Jen will go away.

"Jen, leave her alone." The voice is Pamela Roberts'.

Emilia is grateful to Pamela but hates the way Pamela's smooth hair flips up so easily above her collar. She hates the way Pamela casually pushes up her sleeves to reveal a slim gold watch on one tanned wrist, a thin gold bracelet on the other; she hates the way she throws her head back when she laughs. Her neck is long and smooth, a stem.

Emilia is on the stairwell one day on the way to Geography when Jen's fat fingers creep towards her elbow.

Emilia shrinks away. "Go to hell, you stupid cow," she yells. "Go to hell." Her voice bounces back at her.

Sister Consuelo is behind them. She breathes hard, folds her hands inside her long sleeves. Her round face is red.

"Emilia," she says. "There is little hope for you. Come with me." She leads Emilia into the chapel, orders her to say the Sorrowful Mysteries of the rosary.

"Reflect on the pain you have caused."

Emilia heads for the water fountain when Sister Consuelo leaves. She rummages through her pockets, pulls out the container of pills, swallows them by the handful. She returns to the chapel and sits down on one of the polished benches.

She loves the chapel. The stillness, the light that filters all colours through the stained glass windows, the scent of wax. The trace of incense that fills her nostrils.

—

"How could you?" her mother says. Emilia is in a bed with metal bars on each side. She is looking up at a white ceiling. Everything is white—the walls, the sheets. Her mother grips a bar, rattles it. "What will everybody think now?"

Three days later they say she is ready to go home, although she must keep a weekly appointment with Dr. Roberts. When they pulled her back from the long warm tunnel in which she wanted to stay forever, Dr. Roberts' marble-blue eyes were staring down at her. She remembered him from church. She remembered Mrs. Roberts' pink-tipped fingers clutching his arm, his beige scarf slung casually around his neck.

"Why?" he asked.

Emilia shrugged, turned her face away.

"I don't know how I'm ever going to face Mrs. Roberts again," her mother moans. "The shame. I won't say anything to her, I suppose. But I'm sure Dr. Roberts will take good care of you. Do not bring any more shame on us. Do you hear?"

Her first appointment is after school. She sits in the high-backed chair opposite Dr. Roberts' desk.

"Tell me about yourself, about your family," he says.

She is silent. He waits. "I have a mother and father," she says, finally. "Twin brothers. They are in the army. They are stationed in Germany."

"Well, it's a start." He smiles. He runs his eyes up and down her legs. "Anything else?"

She shakes her head.

"You're sure? Do you have a boyfriend?" he asks.

She shakes her head again.

"A beautiful girl like you?"

She lowers her head, smooths her hair across her cheeks.

"I have a daughter your age. She's in your class at school. She has mentioned you."

Emilia continues to smooth her hair over and over with the palms of her hands.

"Come on," he says. He glances at the papers on his desk. "Come. I'll drive you home. It seems you live only a few blocks from my house."

She is silent in the car. She sinks back in the large leather seat, stares out of the window. They glide past cars that honk, past lights that flicker in the dusk.

When they draw up beside Emilia's house, Dr. Roberts leans over to open the door for her with one hand, lifts her skirt with his other hand and places it on her knee.

She is immobile. She stares out the window at a very bright star. A planet.

She wonders if anyone lives there.

How can you get up there in the first place?

Dr. Roberts removes his hand from her knee, pushes the door open. "Same time, same day next week," he says. "Don't forget."

The curtain twitches as Emilia walks up the path. Through the half-moon glass in the door she sees her mother scurry down the hall.

"You're early." Her mother smiles. "The bus must have raced along."

"Dr. Roberts drove me home."

"How nice. What a nice man."

"Do you remember," Emilia says as she removes her coat, "that Masai man who brought me back when I was little and I ran away? The day after the St. George's Day celebration?"

She is thinking of the man's warm smell, like a soft friendly animal's, the strong arms that hoisted her high, the beads that pressed against her face and made her dizzy and happy with their colour. Red, blue, yellow, orange.

She faces her mother. "The Masai man with the smiling eyes. I wanted him to take me to his home, you know. They sat around the fire in the evenings, singing. Children, adults, everyone. Do you remember seeing the fires?"

Her mother snatches her coat, drapes it over a hanger in the closet. "Emilia," she cries. "What on earth are you talking about? I swear I do not understand you."

"Do you remember that stupid poster of St. George at the school?" Emilia's voice is high. Her cheeks are hot. "His sword was bigger than he was. Maybe that's the way it's supposed to be. What do you think?"

"Oh, for heaven's sake. Come, chop the vegetables."

Her father yells from the living room. Through the open door Emilia can see the paraphernalia of war—the medals, the pictures, the newspaper cuttings, stacks of dusty scrap books.

"What's going on?"

"Nothing," Emilia shouts back.

She smiles. Again she sees the child in a straw hat, pale hair fluttering over her shoulders, the child who did not finish her journey, who lay down by the river and slept.

She grabs her coat back from the closet.

"Now where are you going?" her mother asks.

"I'm going down to the river."

"Don't get too close," her father said the day they moved in. "It looks shallow but it's deep and the current is fast. If you fall, you've had it. And the banks are slippery."

You run wherever you can, her mother has said.

If you don't have a sword bigger than yourself, you'd better, Emilia thinks. She steps out of the back door, runs, slides down the riverbank and laughs, and laughs.

NAIROBI

A parachute, Alicja thinks, as the young woman in the aisle slips what looks like a puffy mustard-yellow vest over her head. The woman is wearing a navy dress, and her red-tipped fingers skim over strings and pockets of the vest. Her voice is clear and high above the rising whine of the engines, and Alicja lifts her doll to the window and moves one of the doll's arms up and down as she whispers, "Good-bye Nairobi. And good riddance."

"Alicja!" Her mother's voice is a hiss. The man on her mother's right lowers his paper and glances in their direction. Her mother gives him a quick, wide smile. Showing me up again, she will say later to Alicja, when they get off the plane and there is no one around to hear or see her grip Alicja's arm and dig her nails in, hard as a cat's claws. A girl of nine, playing with dolls, talking to herself. Alicja had hidden the doll in the school satchel she is carrying as hand luggage, together with the honeycake her mother had given her, two apples and two marmite sandwiches. God knows when we'll eat again, her mother said in the morning as she sliced the last of the loaf into thick slices. She'd never been on a plane before. During the war she'd travelled on farm wagons, trains and trucks, right across Russia, always running and hiding. She caught a boat on the coast of Persia and crossed the Arabian Sea, to Kenya. The journey was long and she slept on the deck with others who had managed to get away. She was hungry, always hungry. She thought of food, prayed for food, dreamt of food. The sailors on the Persian boat were surly and had to be bribed for a loaf of bread, a bowl of soup. A wedding ring would do, a broach, a shawl—or,

Alicja's mother muttered with a dark look, something else if you were young and a woman. When Alicja asked, "What something else?" her mother told her she'd find out one day. "You'll get your turn, you'll see."

Alicja knew perfectly well what the something else was, but she liked to make her face blank and ask what her mother called *annoying questions*, just to see if her mother would tell the truth, for once. She knew, because some of the boys in the camp would ask the girls to go behind the bushes with them for a shilling, a cigarette, the remains of a lipstick or a piece of jewellery they had stolen from their mothers. The boys wanted to have a look down the girls' knickers or to have one of the older girls take off her shirt. Come on, they'd cajole. Let's see your bumps. Alicja stuck out her tongue when the boys tried to persuade her to go behind the bushes. She thought the whole thing silly. She thought her mother should have stuck her tongue out at those sailors no matter how hungry she was but Alicja was certain that she hadn't, otherwise she would have said so.

But all that travelling was a long time ago, years before Alicja was born. Alicja herself has never been on a train or a boat, never mind a plane. The only journey she has ever made has been the five-mile trip between their camp and Nairobi. On Saturdays she caught the dusty green bus with her mother to the Nairobi market. On Sundays, before her father became too sick to go anywhere, she caught the bus with both parents to Our Lady of Peace, to attend Mass. On weekdays, there was the journey to school on the hard wooden benches in the back of the truck, the canvas cover at the opening flapping like a flag in the wind.

Now, finally, they are going to England, to live with Aunt Roza who had once lived in the camp with them in Nairobi. She arrived in the camp just before Alicja was born, just when Alicja's mother had given up hope that any other member of her family was alive. Roza is her mother's older sister and the only relative her mother has left, besides Alicja. Alicja's mother is dark-eyed and dark-haired but Roza has long fair hair, like Alicja, which she pins on top of her head in fat curls. Her face is round and soft, her lips are full and smiling, like the face of the doll Roza sent as a gift a few months after she moved to England, the doll Alicja is now holding on her lap. Alicja knows exactly what Roza looks like because she has a photograph of Roza and herself, taken not long before Roza left for England. This photograph is now tucked into the side of the satchel, away from the softening sandwiches wrapped in greaseproof paper, oozing brown marmite. In the photograph, Roza is kneeling on the ground, her wide skirt spread around her. One arm is around Alicja's waist and the two heads are so close they are almost touching. *Kochana Alicjo, pamietaj o mnie*, Roza had written on the back, *Pamietaj*. As if she would forget her aunt, Alicja thinks each time she looks at the photograph. As if she would forget the first time she saw the doll emerge from the wads of wrapping paper, with her pink bonnet, pink lace dress, white booties and socks, and eyes like blue marbles that closed with a click when she lay the doll down. As if she would forget that in the photograph, she is standing on Roza's skirt. Actually standing on it in her white shoes and socks, and Roza is smiling as if she doesn't mind and will neither swat her nor pinch her arm, when the photographer turns away.

There have been no other photographs of Roza since that one was taken. No more gifts since the doll. But there is always a card at Christmas, addressed to her mother with the words, *Love to you all, Roza and Malcolm*, and last Christmas, *Love to you all, Roza, Malcolm and Tommy*. A small square photograph of a baby with a squashed face and slit eyes was enclosed.

And now Roza, who married Malcolm, an Englishman with a job, has sponsored them. For as long as Alicja can remember, her mother has wanted to leave Nairobi, to leave Africa, which she calls the darkest place on earth, darker than the Russian labour camps where each member of her family died, one by one. *Sponsored.* Alicja doesn't know exactly what the word means but she thinks of it as being wanted, being loved.

The young woman in the navy dress walks down the aisle to her seat as the engines shriek and the plane picks up speed. Alicja's stomach flips as they leave the ground but she keeps on staring out of the window as the plane dips to the left to make a turn and the buildings of the airport become white blocks scattered over the ground. What holds the plane up? she wonders. What if it falls? Will we have time to put on the parachutes and jump out? The parachutes are under the seats. She can feel hers with the back of her feet. The task of pulling out the bulky parachute in a hurry, slipping it over her head, figuring out what to do with all the strings and flaps, seems impossible. She is sure to get it all wrong. The door of the plane is bolted, too, so she'd have to break the window and squeeze through, into the rushing wind.

Perhaps the thing beneath her seat is not a parachute after all. She can't imagine what else it could be. She wishes now that she'd listened to the instructions instead of waving her doll's arm and daydreaming. But even if she had listened, she might have got it wrong. She still gets English words mixed up sometimes.

From the corner of her eye she can see that her mother's hands are clasped into a tight ball on her lap. At least she is silent, for the moment. No sighs, no tears, no suppressed sobs. Not yet. Scared stiff, Alicja thinks.

With a bit of luck she'll stay scared the whole way and there won't be any dabbing of eyes with a lace handkerchief, no sighing and swooning that will make her, Alicja, want to crawl somewhere dark, where no one can see her.

Since Alicja's father died two years ago, her mother has become very accomplished at swooning. First she sighs and places one hand lightly on her chest; then, she sways delicately, like a flower in a light breeze. Soon, she begins to fall, slowly. Into the arms of some man. Always.

Fainting spells, Alicja's mother calls them. She wonders out loud if she has something wrong with her heart or perhaps something is lurking inside her, growing secretly, choking her insides. At first Alicja was startled when her mother began to talk this way. She thought of her father's harrowed face those last days in hospital and the way his eyes had focused on something in the distance. She remembered something gnawing in her stomach each time she left the hospital and wondered if she had worms like the boy next door who was always getting them, and whose mother said she could see them crawling out at night if she surprised them with a flashlight on the boy's bare bum. Alicja inspected her mother's eyes, her lips, the way she waved her hands in the air as she spoke of her heart or the mysterious thing that was coiled in hidden places inside her, waiting to attack. But her mother's eyes remained shiny as she spoke and her lips lifted slightly on one side the way they did when she was about to smile.

Lies, Alicja thought. Lies, lies and more lies. Like the lies at her father's funeral. When her father was sick her mother would talk to her friend Pani Skiba. I could murder him, the drunk, she'd say. If he was half a man I wouldn't have to kill myself scrubbing the filthy houses of the British for next to nothing. I knew the man was trouble the first time I met him. Why I married him, I don't know. Everyone else was leaving this dusty camp with its rickety buildings and toilets just holes in the ground, heading for a decent place to live. Soon, we'll be the only ones left in the camp. No country wants a man who doesn't have the strength to do a decent day's work.

But at the funeral Mass there were tears on her cheeks which she dabbed with a white lace handkerchief. She was wearing a black dress with small white dots that she had sewn, herself, the previous day, and she was holding a deep red rose on a long stem in her hand. At the cemetery, as the coffin was lowered and heads were bowed, Alicja felt her mother's arm around her shoulders. Then her mother stooped, scooped up a little loose dirt and threw it into the grave.

"Go on," she said to Alicja. Alicja scooped up the dirt with both hands. There were pebbles and a large stone among the dirt and when she hurled it all into the grave, the stone and the pebbles rattled on the coffin. She turned to her mother to see if she was to expect a spanking later for her carelessness, but her mother's eyes were half-closed and she swayed. She swayed again, raised her arm and dropped the rose into the grave. A man standing nearby rushed up behind her, and she fell backwards into his arms. It was Pan Orlowski, a man with broad shoulders and a squat face that Alicja thought looked like a monkey's. He had been a friend of her father and was leaving for America soon. He carried her mother back to the car. Alicja followed, kicking pebbles and thinking that at least her mother could pull her skirt down over her knees. Her underskirt was showing and probably other stuff, too, if someone were to look from the right angle.

Alicja kept a list of her mother's lies in her head although many of them also made their way into her diary. At the beginning of the school year, her teacher at St. George's School had passed out exercise books to be used as diaries. Write about what you do every day, she said. About your friends, your family. She said she would never read the diaries; she simply believed that daily writing would improve their grammar, vocabulary—all their skills, in fact. Alicja did not completely believe her.

Alicja wrote *ARITHMETIC* on the cover of her diary, to discourage snoopers, especially her mother. She wrote her name, *ALICJA NOWACKA*, underneath. She imagined herself a spy, watching her own life take shape on the page. But although she tried hard to see herself clearly, she could only see herself through a veil—like the pale shapes of people, or objects in a room, their edges blurred as if seen through a mosquito net. Others were easy to see, her mother the easiest of all.

My mother is a real joker, she wrote. *She's always pretending to faint.* She erased *faint* and replaced it with *swoon*. Swoon was better. It was what the heroines in films and books did. In a way her mother was like those heroines, with her crimped, shiny hair, her red lips and nails, her high-heeled shoes. Alicja wrote about her mother's swooning at the funeral, at the farewell party for Pan Orlowski and later, for the Skiba family. There was another swoon at Mass one Sunday, when she keeled over sideways against old Pan Sikora, a widower who kept to himself and was said to live in a house with servants on the other side of Nairobi. Pan Sikora held her as he fanned her face with his missal.

Her eyes opened, I saw, Alicja wrote of the church incident, dated Oct. 11, 1958. *I thought she was going to wink but she shut them very fast. You should have seen Pan Sikora's face!!!*

I went outside. I sat on the steps. The steps are white. The church is white. The sun was white. (Honest) Too much white. I had to put my head on my knees.

"We stop at Cairo next, right?"

"You'll see."

The engines' shriek switches to a drone and Alicja's mother grips the armrests so hard Alicja expects them to snap off. Her mother crosses herself, a flutter of one finger between her breasts.

"Is it snowing now in England? Does Aunt Roza really, truly want us to live with her?"

"I told you, you'll see. Now stop it." Another hiss.

Full of bloody annoying questions, her mother always says. But still, Alicja likes to ask them. It's a kind of test to see if her mother is telling the truth about anything except things like what's for supper, what time it is, and whether or not rain is forecast that day. Most of the time Alicja knows the answers but if she doesn't, she can figure them out by the way her mother's eyes shift, the way she lifts her shoulders, the rise and fall of her voice. A game of hide-go-seek.

Alicja stores all her questions and her mother's answers in her head. It's amazing how many she can store. They're like a tight ball of string that you can hold in one hand but if you pull on the string it will stretch for miles.

Her favourite questions are those that make her mother give herself away.

"Why do we go to this church and blacks go to the one across the road?"

They were standing on the white steps of the Church of The Immaculate Conception. The sun had dragged all the dazzling whiteness from the church walls and the steeple. Black heads were bobbing in the heat haze across the road, in front of the long wooden building. A cross rose high on the building, black and stark, in the brilliance.

"Alicja," her mother murmured in her ear, then turned, smiling, to old Father Siemaszko, who had shuffled over, his hand extended.

"They have a black god, that's why," she snapped when Alicja repeated the question later, on the bus. She rubbed a zigzag shape on the dusty window with one finger. "Everybody has a different god. Now don't dare embarrass me again."

Mr. and Mrs. Skiba, their neighbours, were three seats ahead of them on the bus. Mrs. Skiba's stomach had been growing and growing for months and it looked as if she had a football shoved under her dress.

"How come Mrs. Skiba has such an enormous stomach?" Alicja asked, another day. Her mother was sitting on the kitchen steps, plucking a scrawny chicken. A thin thread of watery blood trickled from the chicken's neck and was soaked up by the dried earth beside her mother's bare foot.

"Alicja, for God's sake." Her mother tugged hard at one feather. It wouldn't give. "She has a big stomach because she asked too many nosy questions. And the same will happen to you. Now go get some wood for the stove."

When Alicja was younger she would have believed her mother. She would have placed her hands on her stomach every morning to check if a bump had begun to grow overnight, a seed that would soon grow so big she would look as if she'd swallowed a whole melon. But now she is smarter and knows the difference between truth and lies. Still, sometimes she is surprised.

Being surprised is like being nipped by the Skiba's dog when all you're doing is walking by. Being surprised is like being punched in the stomach by one of the boys, or tripping over a leg someone has suddenly stuck out when the teacher has called you to the front of the classroom.

Years ago, before her father died, when her mother still believed she was the only one in her family who had survived, Alicja had asked, "Why can't we go to England? Lots of other people have gone from the camp. Why can't we?"

Her mother smashed her fist into a lump of dough on the kitchen table. "We can't just pack up and go. We need permission, papers, medical exams. Alone, I could go anywhere. I'm young. I'm strong, but who's going to take me with a drunken husband and a child hanging around my neck? Who?"

Alicja stared into her mother's eyes, looking for the lie. But her eyes were wide and clear and hard as two brown buttons.

Although Alicja's mother is now left with only her sister, she has conjured up several uncles for Alicja. Alicja has refused to address them as such. Her mother could threaten and swat her as much as she wanted. Alicja, however, can reel off each of their names on her fingers: Robert, Lukasz, Marek, Edward and Ted.

Sometimes an uncle was there when she returned from school; or when she awoke and padded from her room onto the verandah, when the flat-topped trees were still dark silhouettes against a silver sky streaked with pink. The man would be drinking coffee at the verandah table. Thin smoke curled from the cigarette he held between two calloused fingers. The top buttons of his shirt were undone and his jacket flung over a chair.

"Say hello to uncle," Alicja's mother would say, smiling. "He's just dropped in for coffee."

And in the coffee, and the *bigos*, and even in the scrambled eggs, as well as everything else she served to the uncle, was a little of the brown liquid that smelled the way the murky ditch water smelled during the rains. Her mother measured it out by the spoonful, from the Coca-Cola bottle she had saved.

"What is it?" Alicja asked.

"Flavouring," her mother said.

"Why can't I have some?" She kept her face blank, her voice pitched to a childish whine.

"Alicja. It's for grown-ups only. Now stop it."

Alicja knew that the liquid came from Baba Jaga, the old witch whose house the children pelted with apple cores and mango stones when they walked by, until she came out with her broom and chased them away. Once, when a group of them was passing by, they found a dead devil the size of an adult's thumb, on the ground near the witch's doorstep. *Look. She shrunk a devil and killed him*, they yelled. *Look, look.*

Don't be stupid, Alicja scoffed. She prodded the wrinkled shape with her bare foot. It's just a dead baby bird. But the others ran off, and avoided the house for weeks.

Once in a while, when another uncle had left and Alicja's mother was done with the wailing and wringing of hands and had begun to smile a secret smile again, she would call out that she was going visiting and wouldn't be very long.

"Where are you going?" Alicja would ask.

"Nowhere. Just out."

Alicja followed. She darted behind chicken coops and dustbins, though she knew exactly where her mother was heading so quickly with an empty Coca-Cola bottle, her head down, her skirt flapping around her calves. Alicja waited behind the thorn tree at the side of the witch's house until she heard her mother's sharp footsteps cross the verandah. Her mother ran down the steps, holding the bottle, now full of brown liquid.

"What happened?" Alicja asked when another uncle left and her mother collapsed in a chair, weeping.

"I did everything I was supposed to. Everything. Someone's put a curse on me. I know it. Make me some tea," she demanded as she wept. "Make me a sandwich. I feel weak. I'm dizzy." She clutched her chest and wondered out loud again, if there was something wrong with her heart, or something growing inside her, ugly and heavy as a stone.

So Alicja rushed to slice bread, boil water for tea. She watched her mother eat one jam sandwich after another. She filled her teacup—three teaspoons of sugar—again and again. She waited for her mother's eyes to change, to become veiled the way her father's had during those last days when it seemed that he had already left them. But there was no veil over her mother's eyes, no distant vision that no one else could see. Nothing but a scrawl of thin red lines from weeping.

After a while, at the first signals—doors and dishes slammed, mutters, curses—Alicja began to hide under the verandah with her doll and a couple of biscuits in case she was to be there a long time. She could hear the click, click of her mother's steps on the wooden verandah floor above, and could see her ankles, skinny as a child's wrists, when she marched down the steps.

"Alicja! Alicja!" she called. "Come home right now. Right now."

When there was silence, finally, Alicja entered the house.

"God will punish you for not helping your own mother," her mother would hiss. "Your hands will wither and drop off. Your hair will fall out and the birds will gather it up and make nests with it and you'll have a headache for ever."

Later, when the storm had abated, her mother washed her face, combed her hair and inspected herself in the mirror. "Am I pretty? Tell me," she asked Alicja. "The truth."

"You're pretty," Alicja replied. It was the truth.

"If only I were alone," her mother moaned, "I could go anywhere, do anything." She turned to Alicja. "Too bad you're too big to tuck into a basket and leave on someone's doorstep."

It was at that time that Alicja decided she would ask her mother about the words she heard when she was sitting on the verandah steps.

"You'd swallow a man up, if he'd let you," the uncle shouted from behind the closed living room door. "Eat him up. Body and soul," he added, opening the door and slamming it shut behind him. He marched past Alicja.

What did he mean? She will ask sometime, but not now. She will save this question for later until the vague shape of the answer growing in her head becomes as solid as a statue, until she is able to tell the lie from the truth.

—

Food appears in front of them on small trays: a slice of cold ham with half a slice of pineapple; three slices of tomato arranged like a fan; a bread roll; something in a small round dish, covered with what seems to be a yellow sauce, for dessert.

"Trifle," Alicja's mother whispers. She knows about British food from working in what she calls the houses of the lazy English. "English people eat it all the time," she adds.

She, herself, who is always hungry, who shovels food down quickly as if this is her last meal for the next week, pecks at her food with her fork, separates the ham, the pineapple, the tomatoes, as if she needs to inspect them.

"Not hungry?" The man on the other side of Alicja's mother wipes his mouth with his napkin, hiding a smile, and Alicja knows her mother's whisper about the trifle was not quiet enough.

Alicja leans forward to look at him more closely. He is white-haired and is wearing square gold cufflinks in the crisp sleeves of his shirt. His fingers are long and his nails are smooth as seashells. An Englishman, she figures. Anyone can tell.

Her mother murmurs. There is more talk. A bottle of wine appears on the man's tray, one glass. He requests another.

Alicja admits secretly that there are advantages to having a man around, especially in the early stages, when her mother is still hopeful.

"Baby," her mother says in the beginning as she takes Alicja's face in her hands, "he's a good man. He has a job. He could take us with him if he leaves—to Canada, to America, even England to join Roza. Promise you'll be polite. Promise you'll behave."

"Promise, promise, promise," Alicja mutters, her eyes on her feet. Sometimes she finds herself crossing her fingers without meaning to, and uncrosses them quickly.

Her mother spends a long time in front of the mirror, twisting her hair into one style or another. She smears her lips orange, rubs it off, tries red or pink.

"What do you think?" She turns to Alicja, smiling.

She pins the corner of a white headscarf on the top of her head and floats around the room.

"Could I wear a veil? What do you think? An old woman like me, thirty-one already. But I never had a veil the first time around."

She dabs perfume behind Alicja's ears as well as her own, for fun. She paints Alicja's nails when she paints her own and allows Alicja to choose the colour. She sets out the bottles in a row on the dresser and doesn't mind if Alicja takes a long time to decide. *Crushed Rose, Flamingo, Passion Flower, Ruby Red.* Her mother has a drawerful of lipstick and perfume, too. She used to sneak them from the home of the English couple for whom she worked. Her job was to supervise the houseboys, the cook and the gardener, to make sure they did their work properly and didn't steal.

And, always, from the latest uncle there are boxes of Black Magic, fabric for a new dress, a silver bracelet or necklace, and sometimes, something for Alicja, too. Once, there was a large basket of guavas and mangoes. Alicja made her mother save all the mango stones. She left them out on the verandah railing until they had dried, then combed the hairy part of the stone and painted a face on each one. When she finished, she had a whole, smiling family: father, mother, daughter, grandparents and an aunt.

"Such a good man," her mother says as she surveys the latest gift.

Alicja hates it when her mother calls one of the uncles a good man, because the next thing she says is, "Not like your father."

In Alicja's memories, her father is holding her on his lap and reading from *Basnie Polskie*, a tattered story book illustrated with pictures of kings in carriages pulled by horses, men in knee-length pants and flowing jackets, women in long, patterned dresses. The only picture that makes her uneasy is the large coloured picture titled *Smierc*. In this picture, a robed skeleton skulks behind a girl who is lying on her bed, her eyes closed. A row of teeth are leering in his head and he is brandishing a scythe with bone-fingers. Alicja always wants to see the picture but as soon as her father turns to that page, she stiffens. She says she hears rattling noises, and buries her face in her father's chest. He smells of soap and stale cigarettes and the sour smell that comes from the bottle that is kept beside him. It's only the wind, he replies, pulling her close. It's shaking up the corrugated metal wall at the back of the house.

But her mother, whenever she speaks of her dead husband, calls him a drunk and a fool and, most often, a liar. Promised her the earth but drank away all they had. Drank away his own life. She knew he was trouble the first time she met him. Why she married him, she'll never know.

The Englishman pours more wine into her mother's glass. His voice is low, unhurried. Her mother thanks him, smooths her hair, thanks him again.

Alicja is not quite sure what it is about the English that makes them so easy to identify. It's as if they've all been cut with the same cookie cutter and have come out sharp-edged, symmetrical and smooth. Everyone else has been made from the bits of leftover dough that have been rolled too often and have become slack and grey from too much handling. The English walk in a particular way, with long easy strides. Each of their words is enunciated slowly and clearly. They never rush to get a word in; they know perfectly well that whatever they say will be listened to without question or interruption, no matter how long they take.

Alicja wonders how you get to be like that. It may be like learning a different language, she imagines, which anyone can do by studying hard, watching and listening carefully. She imagines that her Aunt Roza is an expert, now that she has lived in England in a proper town, not a camp. Roza will be the one to watch. Alicja will imitate the way she dresses, the way she speaks, the way she moves, until she has got everything absolutely right. Then, she'll be safe forever. She'll become like one of those girls from Loreto Convent across the road from St. George's School. The ones she watched as she waited with the others for the truck to take them back to the camp. Girls in navy blazers, pleated blue skirts, straw boaters with a bow on the back; girls who walked a carefree walk, with tennis rackets and satchels slung over their shoulders. Chatting and laughing as they strolled, waving a casual wave as they climbed into one of the sleek cars lined along the street.

Roza lives in a house like the houses of the British on the other side of the river from the camp. Alicja is sure of this, although she has seen no photographs and read no description. Her mother told her that the house in which she worked in Nairobi was full of carpets so thick your feet sank as they did in mud. There were paintings on every wall, and cupboards packed with china and crystal that winked when the sun slid in. From the outside, the houses of the British were long and white and surrounded by gardens crammed with red, yellow and white flowers that gave off a scent ten times sweeter than any perfume.

They descend to Cairo, in blackness, and the passengers must leave the plane for an hour. There are straight rows of steady lights on the ground. A hot wind swirls sand around them as they cross the tarmac towards the low, lighted building. Alicja clings to her doll and her satchel as she walks behind her mother and the man. Her mother stumbles on the sand in her high heels and reaches for the man's arm. He doesn't move away but neither does he help her. Her mother clings to her handbag with one hand and her skirt with the other but the wind whips up her skirt and suddenly everything is showing, the dark tops of her stockings, the pale flesh above it, her underskirt flapping like a white flag in the darkness. Through the wail of wind, Alicja hears her mother laughing and laughing.

"Excuse me." The man disengages himself when they enter the noisy building. He disappears through the smoke-filled air, into the door below the sign *Gentlemen*.

"I'm hot," Alicja says to her mother. "Can I have a drink?"

"In a minute. In a minute."

The man emerges, settles himself on a wooden bench on the other side of the room. He crosses his legs and unfolds a newspaper.

Alicja tugs her mother's sleeve. "I'll get it in a minute," her mother whispers. She walks slowly towards the man and stands in front of him for a moment until he lowers his paper. She settles herself beside him, talking, gesturing with her hands, smiling.

Alicja cannot hear what she is saying because she is still standing where her mother left her, in the same spot. Her feet, she imagines, have been pinned to the floor.

The man speaks but does not turn towards her mother. He clutches his paper, raises it and lowers it again. Her mother keeps on talking.

Alicja's face floods red. Her whole body is hot and itchy but she can't stop shivering inside.

—

For hours, Alicja sleeps and wakes, sleeps and wakes, lulled by the drone of the plane, the sudden shudders like a car crossing a bump in the road. The plane suddenly dips and rises, again and again, like a bouncing ball.

"Mother of God," Alicja's mother mutters. Her face is paper-white.

Alicja's stomach flips. "Is it time to get the parachute out?" she asks.

"Parachute? What parachute?" Her mother's teeth are clenched. "Dear God, the child's gone mad."

"Under the seat."

"That's no parachute. It's a life jacket. Don't you ever listen? Pray," she says, "pray."

A life jacket. What good is a life jacket up in the sky?

What good is prayer? When the first Christmas card came from Roza, showing laughing children building a snowman that had a carrot nose and a long, trailing scarf, Alicja asked for snow that evening in her prayers. Not a lot, because she didn't have mittens or boots like the children on the card, but enough to scrape up from the ground and feel it softening beneath her hands as she moulded it into anything she wanted. She woke early next morning and ran outside. Puffs of dust rose beneath her feet. Above her, the sky was a clear blue arc.

She asked for other things later: a puppy, a bicycle, her father to hurry up and come home from hospital. When she asked her mother why she received none of them, her mother told her it was because she didn't ask properly, the way she was supposed to.

"What's properly?" Alicja asked, but her mother only shrugged.

Alicja's mother rummages in her purse and when Alicja glances at her again, she sees black rosary beads twined around her mother's fingers.

Alicja closes her eyes and lies back. She imagines sitting in the pilot's seat, holding the steering wheel, rising higher and higher above the bumps, until she reaches the pure air close to heaven.

ONE OF THE CHOSEN

Not much to show for eighteen years in England, Luisa's mother says, but she is smiling as she lays out clothes and shoes on the bed and tries to decide what to pack in the suitcases she'll take on the plane, and what to pack in the crate that will be sent on to Canada, where Mr. Frankland is waiting. When her mother leaves, Luisa will go to live with Basia, her mother's younger sister, Basia's husband, James, and their ten-year-old son, Andrew.

Luisa's mother used to work in Mr. Frankland's store in town until early this year, when Mr. Frankland's wife died and he decided he was homesick and returned to Canada to the place he left forty years ago when he married his English wife. Luisa's mother wrote to him. He wrote back. Now they are going to be married. Luisa did not really believe her mother would marry Mr. Frankland. Her mother is forty-one. Mr. Frankland must be a hundred. But this morning, Luisa's mother said she was going to leave the furniture behind in the flat. The next occupants could use it for firewood. It was when she laughed that Luisa could tell she was definitely leaving, in five days' time, no matter what.

Luisa has not said that she doesn't want to live with her Aunt Basia and her Uncle James. She is not one to cause trouble, not any more. She has figured out something important and thinks about it a great deal. Her uncle is not really her uncle and never will be. They are not related by blood at all. If Aunt Basia hadn't married him, they might never have met him. She tried to explain all this to her mother but her mother flapped a wet dishcloth at her and told her to stop talking crazy.

Although Luisa has figured out something else, this time she will keep the knowledge to herself. For a while, anyway. Basia and James are being very kind, her mother says, considering. And it is only for three years, after all, until Luisa finishes high school when, her mother promises, she can come to Canada, if she wants. Until then, it's better that her education not be interrupted. Besides, Mr. Frankland never had a child and would find it difficult to get used to having one around at this stage of his life. When Luisa thinks of Mr. Frankland with his white, wispy hair and the lopsided bow tie under his chin—a different colour for each day of the week—and the way he looked somewhere over her shoulder when he spoke to her and always called her *Laura*, she knows that of all her mother's statements, this one is the absolute truth.

Consider yourself lucky you have such a nice place to stay, Luisa's mother tells her. Basia is preparing the large room above James's dental surgery, in the part of the house that juts out at the side. The room is twice as big as Luisa's bedroom in the flat. The ceiling is high and engraved with a pattern of leaves and twisted stems. There is a large wardrobe, a built-in bookcase and a fireplace on the wall opposite the window. Every room in the house, even the kitchen, has a fireplace. Basia says this is because the house was built seventy-three years ago, in 1890, in the time of Queen Victoria, and was then the only way of heating such a large place.

Luisa will fill no more than one shelf in the new bedroom with her books, and probably less than half the wardrobe with her clothes. She is also taking the navy blue shoebox with *Clark's* written in white along each side, in which she has packed her missal, thirty-seven holy pictures, a packet of razor blades wrapped in a shiny gold chocolate wrapper, her black wooden rosary beads and the white plastic cross which is about three inches tall and has the words, *At the Blessed Grotto I have prayed for you*, printed on the front. Sister Margaret brought two dozen such crosses back from Lourdes last summer and gave one to each of the girls in her Religion class. When the other girls weren't looking, Sister pressed a small round medal of the Virgin Mary on a thin blue ribbon into Luisa's palm. Luisa wears it each day around her neck, under her clothes. Sometimes, Sister lends her books about the saints: St. Maria Goretti, St. Joan of Arc, St. Winefride, all young women—girls, really—and each one of them a martyr.

Luisa knows that Sister Margaret has noticed there is something different about her because she has talked privately to her about vocations. Sister has explained that the word *vocation* comes from *vocare*, a Latin word that means *to call*. To be given a vocation means to be called, to be singled out by God for something special. She herself heard the call to the religious life at a young age, at fifteen or so, the age Luisa is now.

84

"Do you think you have heard God call you?" Sister has asked her.

Luisa thought for only a moment. Then she nodded. *Luisa, Luisa,* she has heard, lately. She was not surprised when she realized that this was the voice of God or, perhaps, one of his angels. Now she understands that God has been preparing her for something for a long time, for as long as she can remember.

Luisa keeps her shoebox hidden under her bed. Her mother does not yet know that her own daughter is one of the chosen. Yesterday, when Luisa returned to the flat after the six o'clock Mass at St. Alban's, her mother, who does not usually get up until noon when she is not working, was standing by the window in her black nylon nightdress, a cup of coffee in one hand and a cigarette in the other.

She stubbed out her cigarette in the plant pot with the crooked old cactus and frowned. "That Sister Margaret and those Sisters Mary whatever-their-names sure as hell give you some strange ideas," she said.

Luisa didn't answer. She was not quite sure which strange ideas in particular her mother meant. Is it that she now says the Rosary each night before bed? Is it her lack of interest in the Saturday night dances at the Polish Club? Does the way she wears her hair—in one braid hanging down her back—offend her mother somehow? Her mother is always suggesting that she have it cut and styled. Don't you have any pride in your appearance? she asks.

Luisa has more important concerns now that she knows things that most people, including her mother, don't know. The things she knows are not ordinary things, such as how many rivers there are in England or what year Mr. Macmillan became Prime Minister, or how the African elephant differs from the Indian. She can never remember about the elephant, anyway. The African one has ears as broad as palm leaves, the Indian has small ones, like a dog. Or is it the other way round? It doesn't matter. Nothing in this world matters, now that she has been invited into the real world, the world of the spirit. *Liar, liar,* they hiss. *Bitch. Whore. Filth.* Their voices are harsh, like balloons suddenly losing air. But they cannot frighten her. She knows they are sent to test her. She makes the Sign of the Cross and orders them to leave. Once, she forgot herself and shouted out loud. She covered her ears with her hands and yelled, "Go away! Leave me alone! Leave me alone!" and her mother flung the door open and snapped, "Luisa, for heaven's sake. Have you gone mad? Who are you screaming at?"

Luisa remembers the exact moment she received the sign that indicated she is one of the chosen. It was one year ago, at the Requiem Mass for her father's funeral. She remembers sitting in the pew, staring somewhere above the priest's head when a sudden burst of light lit up the stained glass windows into pieces of colour as brilliant as jewels. But she knew it was raining. She could hear the rattle of raindrops on the porch roof. The light could not have come from the sun. She looked around but all heads were bent. No one else had noticed the colours and she knows now it was a sign, a message meant especially for her.

Everyone said later that she was very brave because she didn't cry at all that day. She found it hard not to smile, in fact, and scandalize everyone. Her father, who had gone to the White Swan last Sunday afternoon and never returned, was right there beside her, and she could talk to him in her head. And when the pallbearers picked up the coffin to carry it from the church, she could hear angels and demons whispering and shifting around. Some of the demons were in disguise. Demons, she knew, were notorious for their attempts to pass as human beings. They could steal more souls this way.

One of the six pallbearers was Uncle James. He didn't look much different from the other men in his white shirt and dark suit and tie. He was a little taller than the others, perhaps, and he held his chin higher. His back was stiffer because he is, as Luisa's mother is always saying, an Englishman, a dentist, a professional, a respected member of our community. Luisa stared at him as he walked by. He didn't fool her for an instant.

Luisa knows that it will not do to talk about this other world to those who have not been invited to be part of it. They will only turn their faces away and smile behind their hands. They will only tell her that she has strange ideas, the way her mother does.

You'd think her mother, whose older sister is a saint in heaven, would know better. You'd think being the sister of a saint would make her pause and think a little. You'd think it would make her wonder. Luisa bites down on her lip when she remembers the way her mother's face creased and her shoulders shook as if she were trying not to laugh when Luisa asked for black rosary beads, like a nun's, for her birthday last May. Or when she hung a picture of St. Michael the Archangel wielding a sword in the devil's face over her bed. Lack of understanding is a cross she knows all the chosen must bear and she has taken to praying each day to her mother's sister, the saint, for guidance.

Her mother's sister is in the small yellowed photograph that hangs in a silver frame on the living room wall. Basia, the baby, is also in the photo, in the centre. Marysia, Luisa's mother, is on the left, and the oldest sister, the saint, after whom the young Luisa is named, is on the right. The photograph was taken in front of the family home on the farm in Eastern Poland, the year the war began, not long before the Russian soldiers arrived and packed off the whole family to a labour camp in Siberia. *Siostry–Marysia, Basia i Luisa w 1939 roku,* someone has written in black ink on the bottom margin. There is a crease in the centre, straight through small Basia's face and her pale curls, but you can still tell that she is easily the prettiest of the three. Marysia is a tall girl with skinny bird-legs and a thick dark braid over each shoulder. The Luisa in the photograph is short, with a wide, pale face. She is squinting, or frowning, into the camera. She is holding a cloth in her hand, probably an apron because there are strings hanging from it down to the ground.

Good old Luisa, the young Luisa's mother always says of her older sister. She is a saint in heaven. When their parents were sick with typhoid in the labour camp in Siberia she kept Basia and Marysia away to protect them and cared for their parents herself. She was already infected when they died and died herself, soon after.

Luisa removes the photograph from the wall. She tears the front page of yesterday's *Daily Express. Japan struck by disaster: three-train pile-up kills 164; mine blast kills 327, injures 348,* the headline reads. She wraps the photograph in the paper and takes it into her room to put in the shoebox. The three sisters have always interested her. She thinks there must be clues in their young faces to explain each one of their lives, clues to show how and why each one got from *there* to *here.* Each of their faces is a kind of map, if only she knew how to read it.

There is pretty little Basia. Luisa's mother insists that you could tell even then that a man who can afford a big house and many other things besides, would claim her. When she and Basia arrived in England after the war, she had to take whatever work she could. She was twenty-one. Basia was fourteen and was sent to a foster family and to school. Five years later she was a secretary to James. Soon after, she married him. Marysia has not been as lucky as her younger sister. She married a man she met one night in the Polish Club. She was taken with his promises and his smile, and the way he sang into her ear as they danced. It didn't seem to matter then that he didn't have a decent job. That's always the way. The pretty one has all the luck.

As for Luisa, you could tell she was meant to be a saint, even when she was very young. She was always the quiet one, the dreamer. Her mind was always somewhere else.

The young Luisa has lately taken to inspecting the face of the Luisa in the photograph, very carefully. She has noticed something that she never noticed before. The face in the photograph is pale and broad with straight dark eyebrows like her own, the hair is neither black nor blonde but somewhere in between. Muddy-brown is the way Luisa's mother describes her daughter's hair, and this certainly is the colour that would best describe the hair of the other Luisa, the saint. The two Luisas look exactly alike. They could be twins.

This is a mysterious thing. A miracle. It's a wonder no one has ever commented on the resemblance. It's a wonder Luisa's mother has never said, "Good heavens, Luisa. You are just like my sister."

"What do you think?" Luisa's mother calls out. Luisa walks into the bedroom and stands by the window. Her mother holds up a navy woollen jacket with a tartan lining. Her fingernails are smooth and scarlet as petals. She has recently had her dark hair cut in a pageboy style and when she moves her head quickly the sides brush her cheeks. "Shall I take this with me, or send it in the crate? I may not need it for a while. I have my heavy coat." She folds the jacket without waiting for an answer.

Luisa stares out of the window at buildings trapped in the November fog. The fog parts for a moment to reveal a tall factory chimney, and closes up again quickly, tight as a fist. Luisa thinks of November in Canada. All she knows of Canada is the sprawling shape she has seen on a map—something like the drawing of an amoeba in her science book—and that there is a lot of snow, and fir trees and mountains. For several months letters stamped with Canadian stamps and blue Air Mail stickers have dropped through the mail slot in the front door of the flat. Luisa's mother kept the letters in her top dresser drawer. She was working in the *Ladies Sweaters* section in Littlewood's at the time and constantly complained about having to refold the sweaters after customers had pulled them out. She had to wear a pastel pink polyester dress with white piping around the collar and cuffs and the customers were not quite as nice, not quite the same class as the ones who once shopped in Frankland's Fine Foods.

Luisa read Mr. Frankland's letters when she returned from school, while she waited for her mother to come back from work. *Very hot and humid this week,* she read. *I forgot how bad it could be. I have bought a small house on the waterfront. Very pleasant. My life is quiet now.* It was all the same until the end of August when she read, *Please do me the honour of becoming my wife.*

We will be living in Kingston, Luisa's mother said when she told her she had accepted Mr. Frankland's proposal. Kingston is a couple of hours drive away from Ottawa, she added, as if this explained everything.

Luisa makes a steam patch on the window with her breath. The patch is as big as her face. She scribbles it out with one finger. The glass squeaks. She turns around.

"Maybe I can visit you at Christmas," she says. "I get three weeks off school."

88

She knows what her mother will say, but she wants to hear her say it, anyway. It will not upset her. Once, she was full of cracks, like an old vase that was ready to fall apart at a tremor and shatter on the floor. It is different now. Nothing anyone can say or do can unglue her.

"Christmas," her mother replies with a small sigh. "That's five, six weeks away. I'll have been married only a few weeks then." Her neck is pink. The pink spreads upwards, over her cheeks. "Summer," she smiles. "Summer's a good time. The weather is nice in Canada in summer." She lifts out a dress from the suitcase and refolds it. "Remember," she turns to Luisa. "Be good when I'm gone. Don't give Basia and James any trouble."

On a warm Saturday afternoon in July when Luisa was five years old, she was walking with her mother from the bus stop towards the large Victorian house where James and Basia lived. Luisa was wearing the pink dress with puff sleeves and a lace ruffle around the hem which her aunt and uncle had given her for her birthday. They were going to tea. Luisa was also going to have her teeth checked. Her father was to meet them there. He often worked for James and Basia on the weekend when he couldn't get overtime at the factory. He would fix a leaky tap, put up wallpaper, replace a cracked window. Thank God for the extra money, Luisa's mother would say.

That day he was fixing loose boards on the coalshed roof. Luisa and her mother could hear the bang bang of his hammer as they walked up to the gate. Basia was carrying a tray and called out a greeting. She was wearing a flowered yellow dress Luisa had never seen before and her pale hair hung in curls to her shoulders like a girl's.

There was a table under the oak tree, covered with a white cloth. James was sitting in the sun, one leg crossed over the other, reading a newspaper. He folded the newspaper in four and dropped it on the grass as Luisa and her mother walked up.

"Luisa," he said as he rose. "Come to the surgery with me now while we're waiting for your father to finish. He won't be long." He took her hand and led her towards the side door.

He lifted her into the chair and raised it high. He removed his white coat from the hook on the back of the door and slipped it on. Open wide, he said, and rummaged about in her mouth with an instrument that looked like one of her mother's crochet hooks.

"All right." He removed the instrument and placed it on a tray.

She was waiting for him to lower the seat when he lifted her dress and slid his hand along her thighs. He pulled the elastic of her panties aside. His rough finger probed her warm flesh. "Be a good girl," he whispered. His face was so close she could smell the sour smell of the pinpricks of sweat on his nose and forehead.

She began to cry. The window was open and a warm breeze brought with it the sound of Basia's and her parents' voices.

"Be a good girl," her uncle said again as he pinned her to the chair with his free hand.

She cried louder. There was a sound of heavy footsteps and a quick, loud knock. As the door flew open Luisa's uncle withdrew his hand quickly and hoisted her up under the armpits to deposit her on the floor.

Her father was standing in the doorway. "Luisa. Luisa. Such a noise. What is the matter?"

James shrugged. "She has two, three small cavities. She doesn't want me to do them now. I'll do them later, one by one. I'll make sure they're finished before she starts school in September." He reached into a drawer and pulled out an orange lollipop. He held it in front of Luisa like a round, bright sun. "Here," he said. "You were a good girl."

"Well." Luisa's father was still breathing hard as if he had run very fast. There were stains on the knees of his work pants and a long smear of dirt across one cheek. Luisa held the lollipop tightly to her chest. James was picking up long silver instruments from a tray and depositing them with a clink, one by one, into a drawer. His fingers were long and pale and he wore a gold ring with a small red stone on the smallest finger of his right hand.

Luisa's father picked her up. "Well," he said again and turned towards the door. "Say thank you."

That evening, Luisa's mother knelt on the bathroom floor to run Luisa's bath. Luisa was standing naked, waiting, when she suddenly clamped her hand between her thighs and said, "I didn't like it when Uncle James put his hand here."

"Luisa." Her mother turned the taps off sharply. She gripped Luisa's shoulders hard. There was silence. Water gurgled in the pipes somewhere. "Don't tell stories. Don't ever say anything like that again. That's very, very naughty."

—

When Luisa had to go to her uncle's surgery later, a new friend came with her and squeezed into the chair beside her. The friend's name was Lila. Lila's skin was pale and her hair was almost white. Although she was as tall as Luisa, wore the same clothes and her long hair was caught up in a similar pair of thin braids that hung to her waist, no one except Luisa could see her.

Lila slept beside Luisa at night. She sat at the table at mealtimes. Luisa screamed if her mother or father sat on her friend accidentally. Her mother grumbled. Her father laughed. Let the child be, he said. Too much imagination for her own good, her mother muttered. One day it will get her into trouble.

When Luisa started school in September, Lila came along. *Infants 1* classroom was a big room with five low round tables. Each table had six plastic blue chairs. There was a playhouse as tall as an adult in the corner of the room, with two windows and a proper door that opened and closed. The playhouse, Sister Anna explained as the children lined up at the door, was only for the children who were good.

When Sister gave the signal to sit, Luisa sat down in one of the chairs, turned and placed her hands flat on the chair beside her. When Sister came to investigate, Luisa said she was saving the seat for her friend, Lila. Lila was over there, inspecting the playhouse. She would be right over. Lila came everywhere with her, even to the dentist's, where she sat beside Luisa and allowed Uncle James to lift up her skirt and put his fingers inside her panties and inside the soft, dark places. She never cried, even when he hurt her, even when he scratched her thigh with his gold ring, and a drop of blood, round and red as a Smartie, settled on her yellow skirt. And Lila always let Luisa keep the sweets that Uncle James gave afterwards, even the special ones like a crinkly packet of Licorice Allsorts or a stick of Toblerone, her favourite.

Luisa didn't tell Sister Anna all this. She just kept her hands flat on the seat and said, "Lila wants to sit here. Lila is my very best friend."

Sister removed Luisa's hands from the seat. She called her a liar, a wicked girl for making up stories. When liars die, they go to hell. "Imagine the smell of your body burning," Sister said. "Imagine this pain for ever and ever."

"Have you decided what you want to take with you?" Luisa's mother asks.

"Yes. I can get everything in the big suitcase."

"You want these?" She indicates the stack of paperbacks on the dresser that she reads in bed each night. Luisa knows each of these books has a bright cover of some young woman swooning into the arms of a tall young man. The woman has long, wavy hair—red or blonde or black—and always wears a tight dress that shows the outline of full, round breasts. The young man is fair or dark but his arms are always muscular.

"No," she says. "I don't want them."

"Right, then." Her mother reaches for her packet of Woodbines. "I don't know what I'll do if you misbehave," she says. She strikes a match and holds it up to her cigarette. "You won't spoil it for me, will you?"

Luisa shakes her head.

She knows her mother is thinking of other times, when she was younger.

The time she cried when she had her teeth checked.

The time James said she could keep the rabbit a child at school had given her in his garden shed, because pets were not allowed at the flat. The rabbit was black, with two white spots on her back. Luisa called her Susie. Uncle James bought a cage from the pet shop. Aunt Basia gave her a bag of carrots and lettuce.

Luisa took an extra bus from school every day for two weeks to visit Susie. She filled the cage with crumpled paper, grass clippings and twigs because the days were getting cold. She took Susie out of the cage when she visited and walked around the garden, holding her close, stroking her long ears. Sometimes she noticed James in the surgery window, watching.

One afternoon the door of the cage was open. The cage was empty. Luisa ran around the garden, calling, "Susie, Susie." Frost had stiffened the blades of grass into whiteness. The chill air cut through her coat, wrapped itself around her legs. She thought of dogs and cats, of a frozen furry body under a bush. "Susie, Susie," she yelled. The words caught in her throat.

Uncle James was blocking her path. "Lost Susie, have you? Did you forget to close the cage, then?" He smiled. "Over here." He took her wrist and led her behind the coalshed. He pressed himself against her. "Stand still," he said. Luisa wriggled away and ran.

"He let Susie out on purpose," she screamed at the flat. "He did. He did. I know he did." She stamped her feet.

Her mother slapped her hard across the face. "Control yourself," she cried. "You're nothing but a troublemaker, you are."

Then there was the time Luisa's watch disappeared when they were visiting James and Basia. The watch had a thin leather strap and a square, flat face and had been a Christmas gift from them only three weeks before. As they sat down to tea, James pulled the watch from his pocket.

"Luisa," he said softly. He held the watch by the end of the strap and swung it from side to side. The face was squashed flat. The hands were missing and the glass was shattered. "I found this in the hall." He paused. "Luisa, why did you do such a thing?"

Everyone was looking at her. Luisa imagined removing the watch from her wrist, throwing it on the floor and stepping on it hard. She imagined and imagined until the image flickered in her mind, together with the image of the watch lying on a bathroom shelf where she had placed it before washing her hands. Other pictures flashed and shimmered before her. Her uncle's hands on her bare breasts. The smell of his warm breath. Peppermints. *Behave yourself. Behave.* Hands grab her clothes in the dark hall, push her into the empty room above the surgery. Another hand (hers?) lashes out, fingers curved, claw-like. An intake of breath. *Bitch.* Three red lines on the back of his hand. Sound of a slap. Her cheek stings. Her head slams against the wall.

Too much imagination will get you into trouble one day.

"Well, Luisa?" Basia's cheeks were pink.

The curtains were drawn. A crackle and hiss could be heard from the fireplace. The room glowed golden. Luisa ran her forefinger around the silver rim of her plate. There were small yellow flowers, each one no bigger than the eye of a mouse, just inside the rim. She had taken a cherry tart. She didn't want it now. It sat in the centre of her plate.

"Luisa, Luisa," her mother was shaking her arm. "Basia is speaking to you."

"I didn't," she said. "I don't know." The cherries in the tart looked like bumps pushing up under a red skin. "I didn't."

"Then who did?" James laughed. "Fairies? Goblins? One of your make-believe friends?" He touched her shoulder lightly. "You're not saying *I* did it, are you?" He was smiling.

"Apologize." Her mother gripped Luisa's arm. She turned to her husband. "I am so ashamed."

Luisa's parents wouldn't allow James to drive them home. I'm so ashamed, Luisa's mother kept saying as they grabbed their coats. My own daughter. So ungrateful. I'm so ashamed. They sat on the bus in silence. Luisa's mother sat in front, her back rigid. Luisa sat in the seat behind with her father.

"Luisa," he said. "What is going on with you?" His face was yellowed in the sickly light. His eyes were tired. There were hollows in his cheeks she had never noticed before. She tried to say something but no words would come. "James has bought you so many nice things," her father added. "Clothes, a watch, books. Things I could never afford."

⸺

"You'll help Basia with the house and with Andrew?" her mother is saying.

"Yes."

Her mother sighs. "They've been very kind. James insisted they'll be happy to have you. Basia says you've been much better lately. You'll be good, won't you?"

"Yes. Of course, I'll be good."

And she will be, now she understands things she never understood before. Everything is happening according to plan. Her father has gone. Her mother is definitely leaving. She will soon face the test for which she has been preparing all the fifteen years of her life.

During Lent and Advent the Sisters talk about discipline, about *mortifying the flesh*, to prepare for *The Coming*. The girls in school give up sugar in their tea. They go to daily Mass. They give up films or kissing their boyfriends. They chatter incessantly about how much they are suffering. They groan and sigh.

But the chosen must discipline themselves constantly, in extra, special ways. Nuns have thin leather straps with sharp studs on the ends with which they whip themselves. Luisa has read about this in books. The nun strips to the waist, kneels on the floor of her cell and lashes her own back five or ten times. More, if she needs to. Luisa doesn't have a strap like that but she has found other ways. She cuts the insides of her arms with the small vegetable knife. She tries to be neat about it by making the cuts exactly two inches apart and one inch long all the way up to her elbows. She doesn't go very deep, just deep enough for the blood to burst through. When she sees the small, shiny red beads she becomes buoyant, weightless, as if she is about to float away. She used to cut her legs, too, but she won't any more because other people saw the marks during gym. One girl asked her what they were from and Luisa didn't have an answer. She wears her gym sweater now during gym to cover her arms. No one should see these marks. Discipline must be private.

"Here, get some papers and I'll pad the spaces in the crate."

Luisa gets the stack of old papers from the living room. She sinks to her knees and helps her mother tear the pages, crumple them, stuff them between bulky packages in the large square crate in the middle of the floor. *Yugoslav earthquake claims 1,000 lives*, she reads as she packs. *Churchill retires after long career. President Kennedy visits Berlin Wall. Soviet Union puts first woman in space.* She smiles. She is thinking of ants. Scurrying, scurrying.

There's a picture of the Soviet woman above the article. She is wearing a bulky suit and a helmet like a motorbike rider. She is lying back with her eyes closed. There is a piece of equipment, like something a scuba diver might use, in her mouth. The words, *Valentina Tereshkova in training*, are written beneath the picture. *Chalk up another first*, the article says, *for the*

Soviets in outer space. Junior Lieutenant Valentina Tereshkova has become the first woman to blast off and circle the globe. She comes back today after her Vostok 6 capsule made 48 revolutions in just under three days.

Luisa thinks of this woman trapped in her tiny capsule, tumbling round and round. How does it feel, she wonders, to be so high, higher than anyone else, above the clouds, close to the stars and the moon? Was this Valentina Tereshkova afraid? Was she? Luisa doesn't think so. She thinks the woman wished she could stay up there for ever and ever. She is sure of it.

"Luisa, stop daydreaming or we'll never be ready."

"Look." Luisa holds the paper in front of her mother. "The Russians have sent a woman into space."

"Russians." Her mother snorts. "Don't talk to me about Russians. Space. Siberia. It's all the same to me." She stands up. "Well, that's that. In five days I'll be in Canada. I'll write to Basia right away to see how things are going."

"Don't worry. I'll be good. You'll see." Luisa's voice is strong and very firm.

"Luisa, Luisa," her father said to her one Sunday after lunch. It was one year ago. She had taken out her school books and was sitting at the table. Her mother was clattering about in the kitchen. Her Aunt Basia had complained to her mother that morning after Mass about the previous night when Luisa was babysitting Andrew while she, Basia, was at choir practice. James had been to a conference and arrived home earlier than expected. Andrew was in bed. Luisa was doing her homework. Her uncle appeared in the doorway and said, "So." Luisa raised her wooden pencil case and threw it as hard as she could.

"Luisa, James has a gash on his forehead," her mother said as they walked home. "He said he found you opening the liquor cabinet and when he told you off you threw something. I could hardly believe my ears. How could you? I am so ashamed. Basia is very upset."

"Don't be ridiculous, Marysia," her father snapped. He marched ahead with his hands deep in his pockets.

"Me? Ridiculous? That girl is crazy," Luisa's mother shouted as soon as they arrived in the flat. "Do you hear me? Crazy. Breaks things, throws things. Lies all the time. Remember those scratches on his hand? She's always been crazy. She should be locked up." She marched into the kitchen and kicked the door shut behind her.

"Luisa, what is going on?" her father asked. He moved a pile of school books aside.

"Nothing," Luisa replied. She was scribbling circles, round and round on the back of an exercise book, and suddenly her pencil was making words without her being able to stop it. *Help help help help*, she wrote. She covered the words with her arm.

"Luisa?" her father placed his hand on hers.

There was silence. She thought about herself sitting at the table next to her father. She was one person in the whole universe. A speck. She could fade just as easily as Lila had faded one day. One minute Lila was walking home from school with her, as she had every school day for years, next minute she had disappeared. Now Luisa remembered what made Lila disappear so suddenly. You're bad, Luisa said to her. You're wicked, she shouted. You let him. Lots of times. Even when you could have stopped him, you let him. You will burn in the fires of hell.

She lowered her head over her books. "Nothing," she whispered to her father. "Nothing."

Her father rose. She heard the front door open and close.

"He must be at the White Swan," her mother said hours later. "Go fetch him. He promised to fix the pipe under the sink this afternoon."

A weak sun struggled through a layer of cloud and grazed her head as she walked. Shiny puddles dotted the road. The street was quiet. A bus roared by and disappeared over the hill. A small green van appeared around the corner and picked up speed. A man came out of the dark double doors of the White Swan. His hands were in his pockets, his shoulders hunched. He stepped off the curb. There was a screech of brakes and the man flew high in the air like a heavy sack. His limbs dangled. There was a thud, then silence.

Luisa knew before she got to him that this was her father. There was no blood. He was lying still on the side of the road, one arm under his head, as if he had decided to take a nap.

Luisa will help with the housework at her aunt's and uncle's house and she will keep her own room very clean and neat and bare as the nun's cell she saw the other day. She sneaked into the private part of the convent with three other girls after school when the nuns were in chapel. The girls had been reading *I Leap Over the Wall* and *The Nun's Story* and wanted to know if nuns wore bras and if it was true that they wore long, loose gowns when they bathed so they could not see their own naked bodies.

The cell was small and square with a tidy bed, a *prie-dieu*, a closet, and a crucifix on the wall: Christ on the cross, to ward off evil spirits. The girls crowded in the doorway. They did not dare step inside and look in the closet where the answers to their questions might be.

"Nothing," one of the girls whispered. "It's boring."

Nothing, the others agreed, disgusted. They padded away.

Luisa, Luisa, someone called. Luisa left the group and walked back to the cell. *Here. Over here.* She stared inside. "Where?" she said out loud. "Where?"

"Are you crazy?" A girl grabbed her arm. "Talking to yourself. Come on. We'll get caught."

Luisa watches the nuns carefully these days. She imitates the way they fold their hands in prayer. She whispers the *Angelus* with them when the bell clangs at noon. Nuns have only one foot left in the door of this world. Maybe not even a foot. Perhaps only a toe or two. Their faces are turned in the other direction. No wonder they are calm, and move as silently as moons navigating the planets.

Now that Luisa is also standing at this door, she prays every day that God will soon give her the signal to step inside. The other day when she was clearing out the bathroom she found an unopened packet of her father's razors beneath the sink. She opened the packet and pulled out one razor and made three small nicks inside each arm. The razors are better than the vegetable knife. The knife is blunt and sometimes she has to cut the same place more than once. And when she forgets to return the knife to the kitchen her mother starts opening drawer after drawer and accuses her of being untidy. The nicks that she made with the razor were not very deep, just deep enough for the blood to gush through in small scarlet spurts, like half a dozen tiny mouths opening. She inspected the wavery blue veins on the insides of her wrists. They were as thin and pale as threads. She wrapped the packet of razor blades in the gold chocolate wrapper and slipped it into her shoebox for later.

Luisa stares in the mirror over her mother's dresser. She moves her head this way and that.

"Do you think I look like Luisa, your sister?" she asks.

"For heaven's sake." Her mother stubs out her cigarette in the ash tray. "How am I supposed to remember what she looked like? She's been dead twenty-one years. What brought this on?"

"Oh, nothing, really."

What do saints look like, anyway? she wonders. In the photograph, Luisa looks quite ordinary. A saint, a martyr, could be someone you pass on the street, an old man or woman, a mother or father, or the girl in a photograph who has been called out in the middle of washing the dishes and is still holding on to her apron. A saint looks the same as anyone else, until she faces the final test.

St. Joan of Arc praised God even as she was burning at the stake.

St. Winefride called God's name as she was beheaded, and a fountain sprang up on the exact spot her head touched as it fell to the ground.

"Here." Her mother lifts up Luisa's braid. "If you cut your hair short, just below the ears and backcomb it on top you'll look really nice."

Luisa stands still and allows her mother to undo her braid, to fluff up the hair on top of her head.

"Luisa? What do you think?"

Luisa is smiling into the mirror. Her features shift, and return into focus. *Open your heart and mind to do the Lord's bidding*, Sister Margaret says.

Luisa is ready. Her heart flutters in her chest, like a startled bird.

SUMMER FAIR

"Shall I leave Dad's supper in the oven?" Magda turned towards the window. The lights blinked, scattering sickly-yellow puddles over the street.

"He'll not be fit to eat by now," her mother replied. She opened the oven, pulled out the dish of fish, chips, a clump of soggy peas, and held it out. "Want more?"

Magda shook her head. Every Sunday night she took four and six-pence from the toffee tin on the mantelpiece and headed for Jim's Chippy on the corner while her mother prepared for the work week coming up. Her mother polished three pairs of shoes—her own and her husband's work shoes and Magda's brown school lace-ups—and laid them out against the wall by the front door. She ironed her husband's work overalls, the wrap-around aprons she herself used at the mill, Magda's school skirts and blouses. She ironed all the underwear, including Magda's underskirts and underpants and whenever Magda protested and said it wasn't necessary, she looked up, secured the strands of pale hair that were always escaping from her pins and snapped, "Don't bother me. I need to see everything right."

Magda's father had rushed off to *Dom Polski*—the Polish Club—with Mr. Rzyba and the other men after the noon Mass. He ran down the church steps, baggy trousers flapping around his ankles. Just one drink, he promised. Back soon, he called when he reached the corner. He raised his hat and waved. Magda could imagine him in that dim room, now, across the hall from the classroom where she attended Polish school every Saturday morning. The room the men called a bar was packed with half a dozen small round tables, several hard chairs and a long corner table where bottles, glasses and a small cardboard box for money were kept. A dusty flag—a golden eagle on a red and white background—was pinned to one wall. The eagle wore a jewelled crown and its wings were outstretched as if it were about to fly.

"Old soldiers," her mother snorted. "Talk, talk. It's all finished. It's been over for years, and still they talk as if it was yesterday." She covered the dish she was holding with a bowl and shoved it on the window sill. "Tomorrow he'll be sick again."

"But he promised to make the doll's bed today," Magda said. "I have to have it for needlework in the morning. Definitely," she added. "Sister says I'm not allowed to start the sheets and pillowcase until I bring the bed."

"Why did you even bother asking him? You know what he's like." Her mother pulled out the basket of folded laundry from under the table. "His foreman won't stand for it. Last time I dropped in to tell him your father's ulcers were playing up, he said, *Right. Once more, and he's finished.*" She dragged the ironing board and the iron from the closet.

Magda turned to the window again and rubbed a circle in the steam with one finger. Beyond the houses opposite there was only rubble—rotting wood, bricks, scraps of metal—from the houses that had been demolished. Their street was next. Magda's parents had received a letter from the Council three months ago, telling them that the houses on this street had been condemned. The family would be rehoused. Where? Magda had wanted to know. God knows, her mother replied and held the letter out for Magda to read, to make sure she had got it right. In a flat, probably, in one of those tall grey buildings they're throwing up everywhere. Prisons, windows like slits. She folded the letter in four and rubbed her eyes with her knuckles, like a child.

Several families from the area had already moved to one of the new housing estates. Mr. and Mrs. Rzyba, who had once lived around the corner, bought a new house last Christmas and the first time Magda's mother had visited, she'd brought back a report. Clean pink brick, a patch of lawn in front. Room for a border of pansies, daisies, even roses under the front window. A row of carrots, another of cabbages and beets in the back. A bathroom upstairs. A toilet indoors so there was no running to the outhouse at the end of the yard in the middle of the night, the wind biting your bare ankles. Everything clean and tidy and white inside. Moved on, she had added, her voice tight. Moved up.

Everyone knew that rats lived in the rubble of the demolished houses and sneaked into the remaining buildings at night. Some nights Magda was sure she heard faint scratching in the walls as she lay in bed, propped up on pillows, the light on so she would be ready when they came. But what would she do if she saw a rat with its long, thin tail trailing over the worn linoleum like a wet string? What would she do if the rat jumped on her bed and faced her, with hard, bright eyes? She could cover her head with her blankets. She could scream, but what would be the use? The rat would keep on staring, waiting. Witold Rzyba would know what to do. Witold, her one friend, had the answers to everything.

She had to be careful these days when she spoke of Witold. Hush, her mother whispered, and crossed herself when Magda mentioned his name. You must not speak of him as if he were still alive. It makes people nervous. He's with God now. The funeral was weeks ago. Remember?

Two weeks and two days ago, Magda corrected her mother, only this morning. The school had been closed the day of the funeral so the teachers and pupils could attend the Requiem Mass. That day seemed like a holiday because the night drizzle stopped and the sun slid out from between the clouds and glistened on the street puddles. Magda wore her lemon Easter dress and, on her wrist, the bracelet of red glass beads that Witold had won at the fair. The beads glittered like real jewels when she held up her wrist to the sun. She wore the bracelet only on Sundays and holidays; the rest of the time, she kept it in a small tobacco tin that also held a photograph of her father holding her when she was a baby. In the photograph she was wrapped so tightly in a blanket she was just a cocoon with a smudge for a face, but her father's face was clear. He was laughing, his mouth open. Your mother took the photo, he'd told Magda. I was laughing and telling her to hold the camera straight or the pair of us would look as if we were tipping over.

"Your father will crawl straight upstairs when he gets in," Magda's mother said.

"Do I have to stay home tomorrow, then? To look after him?"

Last time Magda stayed home from school, her father coughed blood over the sheets and she ran to the phone booth on the corner to call the doctor. The doctor came quickly and spent an hour upstairs. He stopped at the front door on his way out. His eyebrows came together in one line. "Next time," he said, "he'll leave this house feet first."

"I'll write a note now, shall I?" Magda turned to her mother. "You can sign it and drop it off at school on your way to the mill in the morning." *Dear Sister Veronica,* she would write. *Magda is absent today because she is sick.* "Sister gets cross with me all the time. 'You're always absent on Mondays,' she says."

"No." Her mother's voice was sharp. "No. You go to school tomorrow, same as usual. Let him look after himself." She licked her finger and flicked it against the warming iron. She sprinkled water over the apron she had laid out. Head bent, she began to sweep the iron back and forth. There was a hiss, like an intake of breath. Steam rose in the air.

Magda imagined trudging to school without the doll's bed. Her father would be upstairs, alone. He would cough and vomit when she left. Red stains would appear over the pillow, over the white sheets. They would spread and spread, stains as bright and thick as poppies on the hills of Monte Cassino. Her father had fought there once and was always talking about it, to anyone who would listen. Magda would have to make up another excuse to Sister Veronica about the doll's bed, and the other girls would whisper and smirk behind their hands. She would have detention after school but when Sister would finally let her go, Witold would be waiting for her, no matter how late it was. She would not be able to see him, but she would know he was there and she'd talk to him as she walked home. Witold is an angel now, Sister Veronica had said, and he is at peace.

Magda wondered what Witold looked like as an angel. Angels were invisible. They could fly, could go anywhere in this world and beyond. In pictures, their hands were either joined in prayer or spread out, palms up, as if they were calling someone over. They floated in a bubble of soft light. Their faces were always earnest and calm, like Witold's in the photograph that his parents had set up on a small table in the corner of their living room. The table was covered with a lace cloth and the photograph was in the centre, flanked by two jam jars packed with tight white and yellow roses his mother had made from thin wire and stretch tissue paper. A votive candle in a blue holder flickered day and night in the front. Witold's dark hair was parted at the side, the parting as straight as a pencil. The hair lay very flat on his head, as if he had spent a long time smoothing it down with Brylcreem. He was wearing a white shirt and his striped Sunday tie, the one he wore last summer, the first day of the fair.

On a Sunday afternoon last June, Magda and Witold and their parents headed for the park to listen to the first concert of the season. They could see the musicians ahead, at the park gates, struggling out of a van with shiny trumpets and other instruments in huge, dark cases. Beyond the park walls, the scarlet roof of the bandstand rose like a pointed hat.

"Fair's here," Witold whispered. He grabbed Magda's wrist and pulled her back as the adults walked on. He removed his tie and stuffed it in his pants pocket, unbuttoned his shirt cuffs, rolled up his sleeves. He pointed up, beyond the park, to Mullin's Hill.

Yellow, blue and red caravans the size of toys were dotted over the top of the hill, merry-go-rounds and coloured tents and a ferris wheel in the centre. When the adults had crossed the road and passed through the gates, Magda and Witold turned and raced towards Mullin's Hill. At the top of the hill they stopped to catch their breath and peered over the brick wall that ran along the edge. The lawns of the park below were sliced into small pieces, like a jigsaw, by the gravel paths. The pond behind the bandstand was round and smooth and shiny as a bottletop. No sweet-wrappers from that height, no cigarette packets floating on top, no slime. People scuttled like insects towards the benches or splayed themselves out on rugs over the lawn. The large, grimy 'L' beyond the park walls was the school. The chimneys of the cotton mills were tall, blackened needles poking through the town. The Polish Club, which had once been a warehouse and had a long flat roof, could have passed for a landing strip.

They rummaged in their pockets and Witold came up with one sixpence. Magda had nothing. First they watched the bumper cars with their squealing passengers, then the roller coaster. They moved to the coloured horses, tails flying as they danced around. The ground shook to the rhythm of the pounding music and the air was filled with the too-sweet scent of candy floss and the grease-and-vinegar smell of fish and chips.

They pushed their way through the crowd and headed towards the ferris wheel. The breeze whipped up by the whirling wheel touched their faces as they leaned on the metal railing and stared at the screaming, laughing riders. Skirts, coats, hair, flew like kites. "Next summer," Witold moved close to Magda and shouted in her ear, "I'll have lots of money and we'll have ten rides on the ferris wheel, one after the other. You'll see."

He used his sixpence on a game of darts and won a prize. "Go on," he nudged Magda, when the man behind the counter pointed to the tray. "Pick anything."

Magda chose the bracelet of clear red beads strung on elastic. When she held it up, the fair lights shone right through.

"Will your Dad be mad with you for taking off?" she asked as they walked home through the dusky streets. Lights were appearing in windows, curtains were being tugged. Magda was thinking of the long purple-red marks she sometimes saw on Witold's arms and legs, and she imagined Mr. Rzyba unbuckling his belt.

Witold shrugged. Sometimes he skipped school and went tramping on the moors until dark.

"What's there, on the moors?" Magda asked. She imagined a roller-coaster of green hills and valleys, going on for miles.

"Grass and sheep, scraggy rocks. Mist," Witold said. "Sometimes the clouds drop right down and hide the tops of the hills. Sometimes they open up a bit and all this light shoots down and makes everything look like you're on another planet." He stopped and stared at her. "Come, next time," he said. "I dare you."

She nodded. "All right," she answered slowly. But Witold shifted his eyes sideways and she knew that he didn't believe her.

"I'm almost thirteen," he said. "I'm saving up so next year I can leave. I'll get a job with the fair and I'll travel all over the place."

He kicked a pebble hard across the street. "Dad will be sorry when I'm gone."

—

Early in the year, Witold began to be absent from school for a week or two at a time. One day, Magda's mother said Witold was sick and had to stay in hospital for a while. Witold had been in hospital for three weeks when Sister Veronica explained to the class at morning prayer that Witold would not be coming back for a long time because there were bad cells in his blood that were making him sick. She joined her hands and said, "Let us pray for our dear friend, Witold."

Near the end of the day, Sister asked each child to make a card for him. She handed out sheets of blank paper, demonstrating first how each was to be folded in half, with the edges meeting perfectly. Draw a picture of a train on the front, a car, an airplane, a cricket bat and ball, or something else that Witold was sure to like, she ordered. The picture must be coloured red, orange or yellow. Green was good also, as long as it was as bright as an apple. A cheerful poem, a riddle, best wishes or a joke should be written inside. She intended to take the cards to the hospital herself.

Magda chewed the end of her pencil while Sister passed out sheets of white paper. After that Sunday last summer when she and Witold had sneaked off to the fair, Witold wouldn't tell her what happened when he returned home, but she was sent to bed without any supper. She'd stood by her bedroom window for a long time that evening and watched the lights of the fair on Mullin's Hill, the ferris wheel lit up in the centre, spinning round and round like a huge, wild star.

Magda folded her paper carefully, the way Sister had demonstrated. She chose a thick black crayon and drew a large ferris wheel on the front of her card with twenty black, pear-shaped raindrops falling down. *Hurry up or you'll miss the summer fair,* she wrote inside.

104

"What's this?" Sister held up Magda's card from the pile on her desk. "A circle? Some kind of wheel? What are these black marks? Tadpoles?" Everyone began to laugh. "Where is the red? The orange?" The laughter grew louder.

Sister Veronica raised her hand for silence. She held up the card between her thumb and forefinger, lifted it high and moved it from side to side for everyone to see. "You are such a cold child, Magda," she said. She pushed the card aside, gathered the others together and wrapped them with a wide rubber band.

Children were not allowed to visit the hospital, but each time her mother returned from visiting Witold with Mrs. Rzyba, Magda asked question after question. Who else was in the ward with him? she wanted to know. Was he mostly lying down or sitting up? What did he talk about? What did he do?

"For heaven's sake, Magda," her mother snapped one day. "I'll tell you all I know, once and for all. Witold is in a ward with five men. He has a bedside table, and the cards Sister brought from school are on the window ledge near his bed. There's a yellow curtain that the nurse drags around the bed when the doctor comes to examine him. The curtain rings make a hell of a racket. Whenever his mother and I visit, he's half-asleep and it's hard to make him say a sensible word. It's the medicine, I suppose. Satisfied?"

"Yes," she replied. But what she really wanted to know about were the cells in Witold's blood. Where did they come from? How did they get inside him and where would they go when the medicine made them disappear? What did they look like? She imagined them as tiny, fish-like creatures with mean faces and sharp teeth.

She didn't ask her mother about the cells because her mother wouldn't know. All I know about, are the things I can see, her mother was always saying.

There was one thing Magda did not need to ask about because she knew the answer already. Her father had been in hospital many times, and each time he returned he complained that the nurses kept changing the sheets and bringing facecloths and towels and lukewarm bowls of water so he could wash. "How is that supposed to make me feel better, inside?" he'd ask, of no one in particular. Because of her father, Magda knew that Witold would be very, very clean. His hair would be combed smooth and his skin scrubbed pink and white.

Sister Veronica would have been pleased by Witold's starched white sheets when she visited, by his spotless face and hands, the slivers of black gone from under his nails. "Cleanliness is next to godliness," she used to say when he arrived at school with his hair sticking out like an old broom, his hands grubby, or when he forgot to bring his handkerchief for hygiene inspection. She would point to the door and he'd slump against the wall outside the classroom, sometimes for the whole morning, and when he was allowed to return, his face was yellowed, like a bruise that would not heal.

The children were gathering their schoolbooks together to take home one afternoon when Sister Veronica clapped her hands for silence. Witold has gone to heaven, she announced, when everyone stopped shuffling. She joined her hands and bowed her head. "Let us pray," she said. "Eternal rest give unto Witold, O Lord."

"And let perpetual light shine upon him," the children murmured. Some girls sniffled. The boys looked down at their feet. Magda stared at the reddened eyes, at handkerchiefs pulled from pockets. *He's taken off again*, she thought.

At Witold's funeral, the children's faces were solemn and soft, as if they had sunk in a little. There were stiff red and white carnations on the white coffin. Thin sunlight was trapped in the purples, reds and greens of the stained glass windows. The priest said the Mass of the Angels. He wore white vestments trimmed with gold—the colours of innocence and joy. The boys wore shirts and ties, the girls pastel dresses. Crisp ribbons perched like butterflies in their hair. Two stiff braids with white ribbons on the ends hung over Magda's shoulders. She had slept with her hair in rollers the previous night and in the morning she brushed it and brushed it and curled it over her fingers, trying to make the ends flip out, the way models' hair did in magazines. She stood in front of the mirror for half an hour but couldn't get it to look right.

Sister Veronica took Magda's arm and drew her aside when Mass was finished and long black cars were lining up to take people to the cemetery. Jewellery is not appropriate on such a solemn occasion, she said. She leaned over Magda, pointed to the bracelet and held out a hand, palm up.

Magda stared into Sister's eyes. They were small and very dark behind her glasses. Magda could see herself in the glasses, a tiny figure in each lens, the size of a small doll. Sister waited. Magda placed her hands behind her back and knitted her fingers together as tightly as she could. Her heart was pounding hard enough to jump right out. Sister straightened, shook her head sharply and turned away. The wooden rosary that hung from her belt rattled like bones.

—

When Magda came downstairs in the morning her mother was standing by the stove, eating a slice of fried bread straight from the pan. She pressed a mug of tea into Magda's hands.

"Well," she said, and glanced up at the ceiling. "He got home. Somehow." She pointed to the pan. "Eat a little."

The milk van clattered outside. Bottles clinked on the doorstep. The milkman's steps were heard, retreating. Magda's mother dragged her thin hair into a coil. She wound a scarf around her head, swept the remaining strands of hair from her face and tucked them under her scarf. Bits of white from the cotton she handled at the mill clung to her coat. Although she brushed them off every night when she came home, they always managed to work their way under her scarf and into her hair, like small worms.

"Get ready for school." She glanced at the ceiling again. "Leave him," she added, her voice stern. "All right?" And then she was gone.

Magda watched from the window. The sky was milky and low. Her mother held her head down against the wind and her thin coat fluttered around the backs of her calves.

Magda made a thick sandwich of bread and dripping, and a pot of tea. She poured the tea into her father's work flask and left both the flask and the sandwich, wrapped in grease-proof paper, on the table. She listened for sounds from upstairs as she gathered her schoolbooks together and placed them in her bag. She poured the last of the tea from the teapot into her father's mug, stirred in milk and two teaspoons of sugar and carried it upstairs.

"Dad," she said. She stared into the dim room. "I've brought you some tea."

There was a thick smell of sweat, of something elusive, the sour smell of a fog, of rotten leaves in a gutter. The sheets were smoothed up to her father's chin as if the bed had been made with him inside. His breathing was loud and uneven.

The doll's bed he had promised to make was to have been sixteen inches by nine, and four inches high. One pillow and two sheets, bottom and top, were to be stitched by hand in neat, small stitches, then a blanket knitted for the cover. Sister gave marks for correct measurement, for tidy stitching, for the best pattern on the blanket. She gave extra marks for an eiderdown, stitched by hand around the edges and filled with cotton wool, to go over the top of the blanket. Six girls had already finished the sheets and pillowcases. One girl had brought in knitting needles and two balls of wool the colour of strawberry ice cream.

The doll's bed? Magda's father had frowned after church when she grabbed his sleeve. Then he smiled. *Dobrze, dobrze*, he said. Easy. Base, sides, a few nails. An hour. Two at the most, no more. One quick drink and he'd be back.

"Will the Club be condemned, too?" Magda had asked her mother the day they received the letter from the Council. It was only around the corner and a short walk past the shops, after all.

"Keep your fingers crossed," her mother replied and laughed.

On Saturday mornings when Magda was expected to attend Polish school at the Club, she ate her breakfast as slowly as she dared. She took small sips of tea and buttered each corner of her toast with careful strokes of her knife. She took small bites and chewed and chewed each piece for a long time. If she were lucky, she would miss the prayer and, if she were really lucky, the poetry reading as well. It was always boring old Adam Mickiewicz, the national poet. His picture was stuck up on the right hand corner of the blackboard, a stiff figure in long robes. He held his right hand over his chest, the way Magda's father did when his ulcers were bothering him.

"Polish school is silly," she had said one Saturday. She placed her knife on the side of her plate. "It's boring. It's stupid," she added louder and glanced quickly at her father. His face tightened but he said nothing.

"That flag," she began again. "You know, the one in the bar. Somebody should change it. It's all wrong. I've seen the proper one in a book at school." She picked up her toast. "The eagle shouldn't have a crown, you know. Not now. Not any more, since the war."

"Magda," her mother whispered and seemed about to say more but Magda's father slammed his fist so hard on the table the milk bottle toppled over and shattered on the floor.

When Magda's mother sent her to the Club to bring her father home, Magda always waited for him in the doorway. Her father would glance at her and hold up his hand. Just one more. He rose slowly when he finished his drink, still talking, as if he couldn't extricate himself from the stooped men raising glasses in air thick with smoke and shadows. Magda imagined that if she stepped inside she would walk through them, the way ghosts walked straight through doors and walls.

Late last night, Magda heard scrabbling somewhere in the house. She was sitting in bed with the light on and a book on her lap. Her nose, her cheeks, her hands and feet tingled with cold. A rat, she thought, before she heard her father stumble in, and she curled up and tried to make herself small. Rats eat you alive, she'd heard. They start with your fingers and toes.

The tea was lukewarm. She stood by her father's bed and placed the mug on the side table.

"Dad? I have to go now. Dad? I'll be late."

Her father turned his head slightly. His eyes remained closed.

Magda walked back downstairs. She slipped into her coat and picked up her bag.

"Good-bye, then," she called. She waited, listening. A pigeon rustled about in the eaves and then, there was silence. She opened the door, waited again, then slammed it so hard behind her the window rattled. "Good-bye," she shouted as she ran down the street. "Good-bye, good-bye, good-bye," she yelled into the wind.

She caught the bus on the corner, paid her fare, climbed the stairs and headed for the front seat. A drizzle had begun. Water zigzagged down the window. She stared into the glass at a patch of white that was a part of her face, a hollow that was an eye. She had forgotten to braid her hair and it sat stiff and lifeless on her shoulders. She could never get it to look right, anyway. She hadn't even been able to make it look the way she wanted on that most important day, the day of Witold's funeral. Now she understood that she would never get it to flip out at the ends like that, like a smile at the corner of a mouth. It wasn't in its nature.

There were many things she would never do, many things she would never see. Witold tramped over the moors in the mist and found his way back even though every rock, every stone wall looked the same. Sister Veronica said she saw God's face in every flower and in the face of every child. Sister knew that Witold was an angel now, and that he was at peace. And she knew Magda was a cold child. She had known it all along, although on the outside, Magda looked no different from anyone else.

If Magda could be with Witold now she would climb as high as she could. She would see the moors, the sheep and rocks and grass, the whole town spread out beneath her like a map. She would see around every cor-ner, along every street and she would know right away which road led where and how to get there from here. She would pretend there was a merry-go-round under the scarlet bandstand roof, and painted horses dancing round and round to the sound of musical bells. Or that the band-stand was a spinning top, or a large red dot on the map with an arrow pointing and the words *You Are Here* printed underneath. She would watch the red bus crawling over the slick road like a large red slug and she would see her own face, framed like a picture, staring out from a square of glass.